"Is it younger men you prefer?"

Abby's eyes widened. "What do you mean?"

"You said you came here because of Greg. I saw the way you were looking at each other just now. I'm not a fool, Abby, so don't take me for one. I suppose this is the reason he was so insistent that you prepare his case. Is it mutual?"

Abby couldn't believe she was hearing this. "You're crazy. Me and Greg? I'm eleven years older than he is, for heaven's sake."

"I can't see that making any difference."

She let out a little hiss of anger. "If this is an indication of what the holiday is going to be like, then I've made a serious mistake. It will be no pleasure if you accuse me of trying to seduce your son every time I speak to him."

"Let's hope I'm wrong," Hallam said loftily.

MARGARET MAYO

Ungentlemanly Behaviour

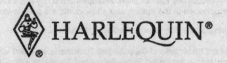

HARLEQUIN®

TORONTO • NEW YORK • LONDON
AMSTERDAM • PARIS • SYDNEY • HAMBURG
STOCKHOLM • ATHENS • TOKYO • MILAN • MADRID
PRAGUE • WARSAW • BUDAPEST • AUCKLAND

FOR GILLIAN

ISBN 0-373-18717-3

UNGENTLEMANLY BEHAVIOUR

First North American Publication 1999.

Visit us at www.romance.net

Printed in U.S.A.

CHAPTER ONE

HALLAM LANE was nothing as Abby had imagined. After talking to his son she had developed a picture with her mind's eye of a stern-faced tyrant, possibly not very tall, completely lacking in warmth and affection, and showing Greg no compassion at all in his time of need.

Nothing could have been further from the truth. Greg's father was in fact well over six feet, fantastically sexy and incredibly good-looking, even though his nose was a little too aquiline, his jaw square and tough, and his dark, thickly lashed eyes had the sort of quality that could melt a woman's bones merely by their looking at her. And at this moment he was doing just that.

For a few minutes Abby had been able to watch him unobserved. She had arrived early for her appointment and his housekeeper had shown her into a comfortable sitting-room that overlooked the vast gardens of the Lanes' mansion home. Father and son were somewhere outside and she would fetch them, the woman had said.

A telephone call, however, had delayed her and as Abby had stood and waited, admiring the gardens through the open floor-length windows, the two men had come into view. Greg had been laughing over something his father had said and the older man's arm had been wrapped companionably about his son's shoulders.

Then Greg had moved away as Hallam Lane said something else, giving him a playful punch as he did so.

There followed a good-natured sparring match, after which the two of them embraced and they had both still been laughing as they'd approached the house.

Upon entering the room Hallam Lane had looked slightly taken aback to see a strange young woman standing there. Now he glanced at his watch. 'Miss Sommers, I presume? You're early.'

'I'm sorry,' she said, and to Greg, with a warm smile, added, 'Hello again.'

He returned her smile faintly and looked vaguely uneasy, but Abby had no time to dwell on the reason why because Hallam Lane was holding out his hand. Abby took it and her five feet seven inches immediately felt dwarfed.

Velvet dark eyes studied her closely. 'Please, take a seat,' he said.

His voice was deep and gravelly and as sexy as his body—a toe-curling combination that added to her confusion. She had come here prepared to dislike him, to stand up for Greg against him, and already in these first few minutes she had not only seen an unexpected *bonhomie* between father and son but had felt a threatening attraction herself! A rare experience.

She'd had lots of dates as she'd worked her way through law school, but no serious relationships, nothing long-term, and in fact had spent most of her adult years trying to prove herself, to fight prejudice and succeed in a man's world. And she had done just that—she didn't take after her father for nothing. She had inherited his fighting spirit and even at the age of twenty-nine had built up quite a fierce reputation for herself.

Abby enjoyed being a solicitor: she enjoyed the variety of work; she enjoyed fighting for justice. Each case she took on was a fresh challenge, a personal challenge, and, although it had not been planned, young people had become her speciality—probably because she was still young herself and found it extremely easy to develop a rapport with them.

When Greg came to see her she had liked him on sight and immediately agreed to handle his case, but he had suggested that she meet his father first, said he would need his parent's approval. 'I think, when he suggested I use your firm, he thought that Sommers was a man,' he had said wryly. 'My father is actually very much against professional women. You'll need to persuade him that you're the right person.'

When she'd pointed out that at eighteen he did not need his father's permission he had shrugged wistfully. 'I'd rather not go against him.'

This was when Abby had drawn up a mental image of a browbeating little man. Little men were always the worst, she had found in the course of her profession; it was as though they had something to prove. Not for one fleeting moment had she expected to be confronted by this physically perfect male specimen.

He had thick black hair frosted with silver at the temples and above his ears, and beneath a black cashmere sweater and black worsted trousers was the suggestion of hard muscles—a man in the prime of his life, a man who took good care of himself.

He sat down opposite her and Greg took a seat next to his father. There was no resemblance between them; Greg had mid-brown hair, quiet grey eyes and a gentle face—he would never stop a woman's heart just by looking at her. She presumed he took after his mother and wondered why the woman wasn't present.

Hallam Lane, on the other hand, had 'sexy male animal' stamped all over him, and together with an air of wealth and authority it was enough to stop any girl dead in her tracks.

Abby found her eyes drawn to his mouth, to wide, generous lips that suggested further lethal sensuality. They were the most kissable lips she had ever seen, and as she and Hallam Lane sat there for a second or two weighing each other up she unconsciously touched the tip of her tongue to her own lips—and it was only when she saw his faint frown that she realised what she was doing and that he was putting the wrong interpretation on it.

Shaking off the alien feeling of attraction towards this big man, Abby became all businesswoman, sitting up that little bit straighter, glad she had dressed for the part today. Often, in her office, she wore something casual— young clients were not so intimidated that way—but this morning, in order to impress Greg's father, she had put on one of her severely cut suits that she normally saved for court appearances.

Her long, deeply waved Titian hair was pinned into a French pleat so that it was tidy and out of the way. She wore no earrings—in fact nothing in the way of jewellery except a garnet ring that had belonged to her mother—and only the very minimum of make-up.

She had thought, when she'd checked in the mirror before leaving the house, that she looked every inch a conservative, responsible young woman. Greg's father could not possibly take exception to her. Abby unfortunately had no idea that, whatever she wore, it did not hide the fact that she was an extraordinarily sensual person. Nothing she could do would ever hide it.

'Let's get to the point, shall we, Mr Lane?' Her tone was brisk and completely businesslike, and there was a deliberate blankness in her expression. 'Your son has expressed a wish that you and I meet. He seems to think it necessary to have your approval before I take on his case.'

Hallam Lane nodded slowly, his eyes penetrating hers with an intensity that was unnerving. 'That is correct. You sound as though you find it strange?'

Abby shrugged, trying to quell the awareness that trickled through her veins. 'He is of age,' she pointed out levelly. 'Parents don't usually interfere. Although getting to know you will no doubt help me gain a better picture of Greg and his background.'

'Interfere?' He picked up on that one word, and thick brows drew together. 'I am not interfering, Sommers. I merely have my son's best interests at heart. I want to make sure that he has the best legal representation possible.'

'Of course.' Realising the foolishness of getting on this man's wrong side so early in proceedings, Abby immediately apologised. 'It was an unfortunate choice of word, Mr Lane. I assure you I meant nothing derogatory whatsoever.'

He gave a wintry smile. 'I'm pleased to hear it. But the fact of the matter remains that I am not prepared to allow a woman to handle my son's case. I'm afraid you've had a wasted journey.'

'Why ever not?' Abby had come up against discrimination like this many times before. With her slender, willowy figure and richly coloured hair no man ever took her seriously. She had a bubbly personality, a vibrant, lively face, and walked with an unconscious sway to her hips. No one ever believed that she was a solicitor.

Now she drew her fine brows together over beautiful, wide green eyes. 'Don't you think your son should be the one to make that decision?' Although Greg had warned her about his father's prejudice it still came as something of a surprise.

'Not when it's my money that will be paying your bill,' he pointed out crisply.

It was an unnecessarily sharp retort and Abby took it as a personal insult. Her chin lifted and her eyes sparked. 'Are you under the impression that female solicitors do not do as good a job as a man?'

Unfortunately, as she spoke, Abby felt a pin fall out of the pleat in her hair and she silently cursed. If there was any occasion when she needed to look professional this was it; she needed to prove herself to this man— perhaps more so than with anyone else she had ever met. Before she'd come to the house today she had formed the opinion that he was a hard man to deal with—and already in these first few minutes he was proving her right.

As she quickly raised her hand to check that none of her hair had fallen out of place she was conscious of Hallam Lane's dark eyes following the movement, openly and insolently appraising the way her grey jacket moulded to her breasts as they were brought into prominence by the action of her arm. It was a typical male reaction and made her blood boil.

She dropped her hand immediately but still his eyes carried on their deliberate scrutiny, moving down the entire length of her body, slow inch by slow inch, missing nothing, not stopping until they reached her narrow feet, clad in black leather court shoes.

It was not the normal, casual glance a man gave a woman—not indeed. She felt as though she had been stripped naked, every article of clothing divested from her body. She drew in a deep, angry breath. 'If you've quite *finished*, Mr Lane, I'd like an answer to my question.'

Her clear green eyes were brightly indignant, her lashes, darkened by mascara, quivered—as did every inch of her. She was beginning to see why Greg had insisted on getting his father's approval. He was quite a man, Hallam Lane.

Black eyes connected with hers. 'As a matter of fact, yes, I have no faith in women solicitors. What's happened to Neville Sommers? Has he retired?'

A shadow crossed her face. 'My father died,' she told him bluntly. It had been a black day in the Sommers household.

'I'm sorry,' he said immediately. 'I didn't know. He was a good man. The best.' There was genuine compassion in his voice.

'And I have taken his place,' she added proudly, challenge in her green eyes.

Hallam Lane looked at her narrowly. 'Under the circumstances I would have expected your company to suggest one of the older partners.'

More experienced, he meant—not so pretty and feminine! Her nostrils flared, further resentment beginning to feel its way into her mind. 'And how do you know how good I am until you try me?' It looked as though Hallam Lane was a real male chauvinist; no wonder his son had feared to make his own decision.

'They're too busy,' she declared bluntly. It had taken her a long time to get where she was today—years of training with no pay, and then, after qualification, a year or two on only a pittance. She absolutely refused to let this man put her down.

An enigmatic gleam entered the velvet dark eyes; his

sensual lips gave an odd quirk. 'How old are you, Miss Sommers?'

'Old enough,' she declared coolly, though she knew she did not look her twenty-nine years. She never had looked her age, but no one had ever suggested that she might be too young to do her job. 'I think that the decision should be your son's, Mr Lane,' she added. 'He is more than happy to let me help him.'

Greg had sat quietly listening, but now his eyes widened and he looked at her anxiously, as if trying to warn her, but it was too late.

'I hardly think Greg has any say in this,' his father growled. 'He is already in enough trouble without some incompetent female making matters worse.'

'I disagree,' she said, keeping her tone calm and cool and completely professional, even though she was beginning to seethe inside. 'Greg needs to build up a rapport with whichever solicitor is chosen to represent him. I am used to teenagers and I actually feel that he and I would be able to—'

'I don't think so,' the older man cut in, his voice cooling considerably.

'But, Father, I also think that—' It was the first time the boy had spoken and he was instantly silenced by a withering glance.

'What you think has nothing to do with it,' declared Hallam firmly.

'I like Miss Sommers, though; I am sure that—'

'Greg, let me deal with this.'

Abby could not understand why this man would not let his son speak for himself on this issue. She felt sorry for Greg, more especially when he gave her a pleading glance behind his parent's back.

'I believe,' she said to Hallam Lane, trying to keep

her voice reasonable, 'that my age is something in my favour as far as your son is concerned. I can relate to young people better than, say, Grypton or Evans—' both of whom were well into their fifties '—and I therefore think that it would be in Greg's best interests if I represented him. Perhaps I could have a word with your wife? This should be a mutual decision.'

'There is no Mrs Lane.' His brow was suddenly as dark as a thundercloud and Abby could see that she had touched a raw nerve. Presumably his marriage had not lasted—and if he was always this chauvinistic where women were concerned then she could see why.

'I also think it is time you went,' he added coldly and purposefully. 'You can tell your partners why they've lost my business—and if they have any sense they'll get rid of you.'

Abby opened her mouth to object, took one look at Greg's face pleading with her to say no more, and closed it again. If this was Hallam Lane's decision, and his son was prepared to go along with it, then there was no point in arguing, even though she thought the elder Lane was making a big mistake. She rose to her feet, picked up her handbag and walked out of the room.

Although she did not feel like being polite, although she wanted to tell Hallam Lane exactly what she thought of him for inflicting his personal prejudices on his son, Abby nevertheless held out her hand as she reached the main entrance and smiled graciously. 'Goodbye, Mr Lane; I'm sorry you feel this way.'

Contact with him felt like fire-water shooting through her veins. Despite his hostility towards her he was still a lethally attractive man, and she could not get her hand free quickly enough.

He gave a quietly confident smile as she snatched it

away, almost as though he knew what effect he was having on her, as though she was conforming to some preconceived pattern. Unless it was her imagination.

Abby knew men reacted in many different ways when confronted with a woman solicitor, especially when that woman was attractive as well. Not that she considered herself unduly beautiful; she thought her nose too tiny, her mouth too wide. She was oblivious to the effect she really had on people.

'Greg should have known how I felt,' he said gruffly, eyes steady on hers. 'He shouldn't have wasted your time. Goodbye, Sommers.'

She looked at the boy, feeling genuinely sorry for him because he had seemed to really like her. 'Goodbye, Greg,' she said, and then walked out to her car, conscious of Hallam Lane watching her every inch of the way.

Once inside her metallic-blue Rover she drew in a steadying breath, fired the engine, and moved away so quickly that gravel spurted beneath her tyres. Black and gold wrought-iron gates—set into the high wall surrounding the property—opened automatically as she approached, and Abby could not help wondering uncharitably what this man had got to hide that his place was like a fortress.

Abby was not given to thinking ill of people but Hallam Lane really had struck a wrong chord with her. Apart from her totally unexpected physical response to him—something that she would need to think about later—she had found him a totally unreasonable man.

His disapproval of career women should not have entered into things since it was Greg she had been asked to represent. She felt sorry for his son. He had not been allowed to get a word in. If she hadn't seen how well they got on together she would have retained her initial impression that he ruled his son with a rod of iron. It was all very puzzling.

When she arrived back at the discreetly elegant office buildings of Grypton, Sommers & Evans in the English county town of Shrewsbury, Abby was still frowning over the unfairness of the situation. She stripped off her jacket and tossed it impatiently onto the coatstand, threw the Lane file into her wastepaper basket—there was no point in keeping that any longer—and dropped heavily into her chair.

The more she thought about the way Hallam Lane was controlling the situation, the more annoyed she became. Maybe she ought not to have given in so quickly; maybe she ought to have stood her ground, stuck up for Greg. He had looked truly disappointed. On the other hand, as Hallam had said, he was the one paying the bills—so ultimately it was his choice.

When the telephone rang she was surprised to hear her secretary say that she had Mr Lane on the line. 'Hallam Lane?' she queried, not even stopping to wonder why this man came into her thoughts first.

'No, it's Gregory, I think,' replied Linda.

'I see,' Abby said slowly. 'Put him on.' Perhaps he had been able to persuade his father to think again. Stranger things had happened.

'Hello, Greg; this is unexpected,' she said, as soon as the call was put through. 'Has your father changed his mind?'

'Goodness, no,' came the immediate response. 'But he's gone out and I want to say how sorry I am that I got you all the way out to the house for nothing. I really did think that once he'd seen you he would—'

'You don't have to apologise,' she interrupted gently.

'I meet all sorts in this job. It was nice of you to ring, though; I appreciate it.'

There was a slight pause before he spoke again. 'It wasn't simply to apologise for my father; I—I really want you to represent me. Will you do it?' There was an earnest note in his voice now.

Abby's brain went into fast forward as she realised the full implication of what he was asking. It could cause all sorts of problems if she went against the older man's wishes, and at the very least it would generate friction between father and son. 'I don't think it would be very wise,' she said. 'Your father—'

'This is my own decision,' he cut in, surprising her with his determination.

'Why didn't you make this stand in front of him?' she asked, frowning faintly into the phone.

'Because I respect him, I guess,' he told her wryly, 'and rarely go against his wishes—and I especially didn't think it wise, considering the trouble I'm already in,' he added sorrowfully. 'But I really do want you to help me, and I thought that if I presented him with a *fait accompli* he would be unable to do anything about it. I didn't do that burglary, I promise you. I was—'

'Greg,' she cut in firmly, her mind suddenly made up, 'I will do it, but only on condition that your father is in agreement. Talk to him again, tell him what you've told me, tell him you have confidence in me, that you find it easy to relate to me—better than you would an older person—and then come and see me. Shall we say ten o'clock in the morning?'

He agreed reluctantly and after she had put down the telephone Abby sat in thoughtful silence as she tried to visualise what the next meeting between father and son would be like. Somehow she could not see Hallam Lane agreeing to her taking on his son's case, whatever Greg said. His dislike of career women was so intense that nothing would move him. She did not expect to see Greg again.

Pressure of work soon took over and the Lanes were forgotten. It was not until the day ended and she was in bed that Abby thought about either of them, and it was, not surprisingly, the elder man who was at the forefront of her mind.

It had been a shock to feel any sort of reaction to him. She had built up an automatic barrier where men were concerned, having discovered that most of them were arrogant and domineering and downright dismissive when faced with a successful career woman. Hallam Lane was no exception.

Why, then, had she felt this instant fascination? It could be dangerous, especially if Greg did manage to persuade his father to change his mind. Just the thought of seeing Hallam Lane again sent a flurry of sensation through her limbs. Lord, it was stupid. How could such a thing have happened?

She determinedly switched her mind to Greg, wondering how long he had been without a mother. It could be part of his problem. Had he been a troublesome child? It would be up to her to find out the history of this young man who had appealed to her for help—and how better than through his father?

A few minutes before ten the next morning her secretary rang through to announce that Mr Lane was waiting to see her.

'Send him in,' Abby said at once, feeling pleased that Greg had somehow managed to get round his father. She had not expected that. A ready smile played on her lips as the door opened but it faded instantly when it was the senior Lane who entered her room.

Not wanting to feel at a disadvantage where this big man was concerned, she jumped immediately to her feet and there were no preliminaries on either side. She had his measure now and was ready for him. She barred from her mind any sensual thoughts.

'If you're here to say that you forbid me to take Greg's case then I think you're making a very foolish mistake,' she said firmly and clearly. 'Greg trusts me and wants me and—'

'You're wasting your breath.'

Abby dragged her fine brows together. 'I don't think so. I happen to believe in your son.' Hallam Lane wore a charcoal-grey suit this morning, emphasising the lean lines of his body but hiding none of its strength. She had made no mistake in remembering how destroyingly attractive to her senses he was.

'I'm not here to denigrate you, Sommers,' he said surprisingly. 'You can handle Greg's affairs.' Dark, long-lashed eyes watched intently for her reaction—eyes so dark that they rendered the irises invisible.

Abby's frown deepened and for an instant she felt at a disadvantage. 'I don't understand.' And she wished she had dressed differently.

She wore a softly flared cotton dress in emerald-green which matched the colour of her eyes—and made her look even younger! A fact that she was sure had not gone unnoticed by her unexpected visitor.

Her hair was also unrestrained this morning, falling in a torrent of heavy waves about her shoulders, a flame of red that caught Hallam's eyes and made him frown at her in silence for several long seconds.

She spoke before he could. 'What has made you change your mind?'

'Greg reminded me he is of an age to make his own decisions,' he commented drily. 'Not that I am totally in agreement with that. He has made some tragic mistakes in his young life.'

Even as he spoke his eyes were making a careful study of her mouth, and then they moved slowly downwards to rest on the pert thrust of her breasts, moulded so clearly by the fine green cotton. It was yet a further deliberate appraisal, perhaps designed to see what sort of reaction he got! Abby's hackles rose.

'If it is your intention to use sex as a weapon you're wasting your time,' she told him coolly and defensively. She could not deny that she felt something, that a trickle of awareness ran through her veins, but she was most certainly not going to let him see it.

'Who's talking about sex?' he asked, a sardonic curve now to his mouth, a quirk to an eyebrow.

Abby glared. 'I don't like the way you're looking at me, Mr Lane. In fact I find your whole attitude extremely offensive.'

Never had Abby spoken to a prospective client—or a client's father—in such a manner, but there was something about this man that rubbed her up the wrong way, or was it because she was trying to defend herself? Was it her own sexuality that scared her, the way he managed to arouse her without even trying?

His smile widened, revealing a perfect set of white teeth. 'I'm a red-blooded male, Sommers, admiring a beautiful lady. If you read anything more into it then you're living up to my expectations.'

Abby's head jerked and she gave a swift frown. 'What is that supposed to mean?'

'Aren't all women the same?' he jeered. 'Especially when they work in a man's world. I guess domesticity and a few children around your feet is the last thing you want. You earn good money; you're free to have as many affairs as you wish. I imagine some men find excitement in dating successful career women, but personally I prefer someone who behaves like a real woman.'

Abby wondered what on earth had brought this on. 'I'm sure I didn't ask for any of this, Mr Lane,' she said tightly. 'I think you're totally out of order and I think it might be best if you left.'

She realised that she was jeopardising the chance he had given her of taking Greg's case, but, heavens, she didn't have to put up with his insults. She marched across to the door and opened it, discovering to her astonishment that his son was hovering outside.

Before she could speak, however, before she could even venture a smile, the door was firmly closed again, taken from her by a hand that was stronger and more insistent than her own. She turned furiously. 'What the devil do you think you're—?'

'Just proving a point,' he muttered, and she was pulled against the hardness of his body, immobilised by one firm hand behind her back and another behind her head. His lips unerringly found hers.

Abby was taken so much by surprise that for the first few seconds she was frozen, simply standing there and allowing the kiss, insane though it was. When finally she came back to life and began to fight, pummelling her fists against a rock-hard body, demanding that he let her go, she was perturbed to see tiny flames of desire in the blackness of his eyes.

Also, more frightening still was her own sizzling response to his compelling sensuality. It could not be stemmed, nor could she ignore it. It was by far the most scary thing that had ever happened to her.

It seemed an age before he finally released her—a whole lifetime of drumming, throbbing heartbeats and racing pulses, of a pagan rhythm that threatened to take over her whole body.

'Well, well, well, Sommers,' he said, his full lips curled in confident amusement, his eyes mocking. 'You did not let me down.'

She threw him a swift, savage glance, though in truth it was herself, her own unaccountable behaviour that she was more angry with. 'You're despicable!'

'And you're incredibly beautiful when you're angry—and also completely predictable.'

Abby's body shook with anger; she was furious with both him and herself. 'You're deeply mistaken, Mr Lane. You have no idea at all what I am like. And do you know what? I feel sorry for Greg having a father like you; you're the one who has no morals.'

He smiled—a highly dangerous smile—appearing not in the least perturbed by her harsh words. 'Just remember,' he warned, a steely glint now in his eyes, 'I want no sentence passed against my son.'

She looked at him coolly and disdainfully. 'It depends whether he is innocent, Mr Lane.'

'It is up to you to prove that he is,' he reminded her tersely.

'Is it *your* good name you're thinking of?' Abby knew she was dicing with danger but restraint had long since flown out of the window where this man was concerned.

Black eyes glittered. 'Just do the job you're getting paid for.' Then he yanked the door open and motioned his son to enter. Greg glanced from one to the other and it was obvious by his worried expression that he had heard their raised voices. 'I'll see you later, son,' Hallam growled as he brushed past him and left the office.

Abby could have done with a few moments to pull herself together before talking to Greg.

'It sounded as though my father was very angry,' said the young man quietly.

She grimaced. 'He was.'

'He hasn't changed his mind about—?'

'Of course not,' she assured him hastily.

'Then what—?'

Again she interrupted. 'It doesn't matter, Greg.' Her tone was soft and friendly, her eyes warm. She was in control of herself again. 'Sit down. We have a lot of talking to do.'

CHAPTER TWO

ABBY hoped and prayed that she would see nothing
more of Gregory Lane's father. She was completely confused by the feelings he had aroused in her—angry with
him for daring to kiss her, but even more so with herself
for allowing it in the first place. The whole sequence of
events had stirred her emotions to such an extent that
she could not stop thinking about him.

She found Hallam Lane so undeniably attractive that
it was the biggest pity in the world that he felt the way
he did about career women. He was the sort of man she
could have fallen for, the first one ever to make her sit
up and take notice, who had sent her red blood corpus-
cles into a dizzying spin.

And unfortunately—for her peace of mind at any
rate—he did not keep out of her life. He attended the
initial court hearing and he also accompanied Greg the
next time he came to see her.

When the two of them walked into her office Abby
felt everything inside her flutter into chaos—every
nerve-end, every pulse, each heartbeat. Determinedly,
however, she stiffened her spine, hardened her tone and
went straight into the attack. 'I think you should let Greg
handle his own affairs, Mr Lane.'

Today she was wearing a dusky pink skirt and match-
ing silk blouse that should have clashed outrageously
with her hair but somehow didn't. Instead she managed

to look deliciously feminine. She had taken her hair back into her nape with a big pink and gold slide, and gold hoop earrings hung from her ears.

Had she known that Greg's father intended putting in an appearance she would most definitely have put on a plain dark suit and probably even a pair of tortoiseshell glasses! Anything to give herself a more professional image. Though, she had the uncomfortable feeling that nothing she wore would make one iota of difference where this man was concerned.

Black eyes locked into hers after they had made their now customary appraisal—during which time every single one of Abby's senses raced into action. It was alarming the way her body reacted to him and she wished there was something she could do about it.

'I happen to think,' he said evenly, 'that there is every need for me to be present.' His eyes continued to war with hers. 'And I shall continue to attend until I've satisfied myself that you have sufficient experience to deal with my son's case.'

He sounded so officious, so arrogant, so pompous that hostility prickled Abby's spine now, all sensuous feelings flying, and she drew herself up tall, prepared to do battle. 'Perhaps you'd like a word with one of my partners?' she queried tartly. 'I'm sure they'll be more than willing to vouch for me.'

Greg stood at his father's side, fidgeting and looking acutely uncomfortable. Abby felt sorry for him. He was caught in their crossfire and it couldn't be good for his morale. It was such a pity that his father found it essential to interfere.

'I don't think that will be necessary,' Hallam Lane answered evenly, as she had somehow expected he might. 'But I would like Greg to leave us; I want a few words with you alone.'

Greg looked suddenly both startled and apprehensive, as she was herself, and he glanced at her hesitantly, as if asking what he should do.

Abby saw no reason why he should go out of the room, and she could not think what Hallam Lane had to say that could not be said in front of his son, but she also knew that the man would not go until he had got off his chest whatever was bothering him, so she gave Greg a slight nod and a faint smile, trying to reassure him.

When they were alone she stood tall, chin high, green eyes wary, her fingertips on the edge of the desk, and waited to hear what he had to say. Hallam Lane wore a navy suit and blue silk shirt and tie this morning, which seemed to emphasise his height and breadth. He looked every inch as dynamically attractive as before. Abby found her mouth growing dry simply by her looking at him.

'Did Greg tell you that he has been in trouble before?' he asked abruptly.

With an effort Abby dragged her attention away from the man and back to the business in hand. 'As a matter of fact, no. But he is here again today so that we can further discuss—'

'He wouldn't have told you,' he cut in, a faint harshness in his tone that told her how disappointed he was in his son.

'I beg to differ,' she said quickly and decisively. 'Once I've built up a rapport with Greg, once he realises the importance of my knowing everything, I'm sure he will keep nothing from me. You should have faith in your son, Mr Lane.'

'I must admit the boy seems to have taken a liking to you,' he admitted grudgingly, his narrowed eyes watchful on hers.

'It is important that he should,' Abby replied, surprised and rather pleased by his statement. 'And as a matter of fact I think that you're insulting his intelligence by accompanying him everywhere he goes.' She determinedly held his gaze. 'Why don't you give him some breathing space?'

'Has he complained?' His tone was suddenly sharp-edged, his eyes suspicious.

Abby had not thought Hallam Lane would put this interpretation on her words and instantly shook her head. 'Not at all.'

'But you think that you're in a position to tell me what to do?' he rasped, stepping swiftly forward until only her desk was between them, coal-black eyes boring threateningly into green, using the full power of his body to intimidate her.

Or, at least, that was what it felt like to Abby. 'Of course not,' she said guardedly and quietly. 'It just seems to me that—'

'I'd thank you to keep your opinions to yourself,' he growled. 'How I—' At that moment the telephone on Abby's desk rang and as she lifted the receiver Hallam was compelled to stand in silence while she dealt with her call.

She was uncomfortably aware that he never once took his eyes off her, that he observed closely the porcelain quality of her skin with its scattering of freckles, her almond-shaped green eyes and tiny straight nose, her wide mouth and small, delicate ears.

And as if that wasn't enough he allowed his eyes to slide down the slender column of her throat and rake over her breasts which were accentuated by the gentle silk of her blouse. And he made it perfectly clear that he was seeing her rounded curves beneath and not the actual clothes that she wore.

Abby felt her skin grow warm. She tried to ignore him, concentrate on her phone call. She even turned her back on him but it made no difference. He still watched and she still felt the full power of this male animal who had made such an impact on her.

She hated herself for acknowledging his intense sensuality, for letting it affect her the way it did, and as soon as she had finished her call Abby glanced briskly and pointedly at her watch. 'I'd like to speak with your son now, Mr Lane. I have another client to see in half an hour.'

Thick dark brows rose. 'No one dismisses me, Sommers, until I am ready to go.' His voice was at its most pompous.

She tossed her head, beautiful eyes flashing disdainfully. 'The more time you spend talking, the less time Greg will have.'

A thoughtful expression crossed the man's face; a gleam appeared in the jet-black eyes. 'Perhaps you should come to the house and talk to him. How about Friday evening? Come for a meal and—'

Abby stopped him with a quick gesture of her hand, appalled by the very idea. Go to his house? Sit through a meal with him? Suffer some more? 'No, thank you, Mr Lane,' she said hastily. 'You would obviously want to put in your two pennies' worth and that wouldn't help matters at all. It would be much better if I saw Greg here—and alone.' She paused a moment and then added softly, 'As a matter of fact I think you intimidate him.'

Hallam Lane frowned swiftly and harshly, black

brows drawing together in disbelief. 'Intimidated? Greg? By me?' He was obviously totally shocked by the suggestion. 'What complete and utter nonsense. What on earth put that idea into your head?'

Abby shrugged expressively. 'It was the impression I got.'

'Impressions, impressions,' he jeered. 'I thought solicitors dealt in fact, not supposition. I'm telling you, Sommers, that if my son wasn't so insistent that he wanted you to defend him then I wouldn't waste a second of my breath talking to you.'

Abby's chin lifted. 'The feeling's mutual, Mr Lane. That's why I don't think it would be a very good idea, my coming to your house.' Or was it her own feelings that she was scared of—the fact that he had this amazing ability to draw some sort of unwanted response from her? Was she afraid of what might happen if she ventured into the Lane household?

He came round the desk towards her then, and she felt the threat of dangerous magnetism. 'How else are you going to allow my son enough of your time?' he questioned, his face pushed up close to hers, so that she could see every pore in his skin, the clear whites of his eyes, inhale the male scent of him. 'Half an hour is less than adequate,' he growled. 'It's nothing at all.'

'We could have got through quite a lot if you hadn't insisted on speaking to me first,' she told him abruptly, standing her ground, refusing to back away, although she would have liked to. His powerful virility was again disturbing her pulses to such an extent that she felt sure he must see them leaping. 'You've already wasted a good ten minutes.'

'Which I've no doubt you will charge me for.' Hard eyes locked into hers.

'No doubt,' she returned, determined that she would not be the first to look away.

'Then—since I'm paying for your time—I'm afraid I'm going to insist that you interview my son in the privacy of his own home where there will be no interruptions and no time limit.'

'You'll be charged extra out of office hours,' she told him levelly.

'I understand that.'

'And I shall still wish to see him alone.'

Black eyes narrowed until they were no more than slits in his harshly angular face—glittering slits staring out at her from between lashes which were ridiculously long on so masculine a man.

'I insist,' she said firmly.

Finally the big shoulders shrugged. 'Have it your own way. Shall we say eight o'clock? I'll send a car for you.'

'No, thanks,' she retorted hastily. 'I'll drive myself there.'

'You can have a drink if you don't drive.'

'I never drink.'

Thick brows rose. 'Not at all?'

'Maybe a little wine on occasions,' she admitted. But she had to be careful; even a little alcohol made her light-headed—and Abby liked to be in control at all times.

'And I imagine, from the lack of an ashtray in this room, that you don't smoke either. What a virtuous female we have here.' There was scorn in his voice and Abby was about to come back with some biting retort when he added, 'Why aren't you married?'

She was startled by his question and her chin came up again. 'Let's say I've never met the right man.' There had never been anyone even remotely serious for that matter, but she wasn't going to tell him that. Her mother said she was too fussy, but she couldn't see any harm in it. She certainly had no intention of marrying a man who would constantly try to demoralise her, and they all did that—at least, the ones she had met did. And Hallam Lane was no different!

'If you're not careful,' he warned, 'you'll turn into an embittered old spinster. And that would be a terrible shame for someone as—' he reached out and stroked the back of a finger down her cheek '—beautiful as you.' His tone had gone an octave lower, to a deeply sensual growl that shivered through Abby's bloodstream.

She jerked her head away, but not soon enough, not before she had felt the searing heat of his fingers. Lord help her if this was going to happen each time they met! 'Please get out of my office,' she said through gritted teeth.

A disturbing smile flickered at the corners of his sensual mouth and he did not move an inch. 'Maybe,' he muttered, 'it would be interesting to find out exactly what makes you tick.'

Abby stiffened and glared, desperately wishing that she had never been approached to take Greg's case. When fathers attended with their sons they did not normally take over as this man was doing, and certainly none of them had ever affected her pulse rate!

'You're an intriguing female, Sommers.' The deep, sexy growl was still there, at complete odds with the harsh tones he had used earlier. 'I shall look forward to our next meeting.' And with that, both to her surprise and her intense relief, Hallam Lane finally moved, finally opened the door, leaving Abby with an oddly beating heart and a sense of total confusion.

Greg looked as bewildered as she felt when his father

led him away, and in the days that followed she pondered over this older Lane who had got through to her as no one else ever had, and who seemed to find a great deal of pleasure in taunting her.

As a consequence she was discovering a sensual side to her nature that had not seen the light of day since her first, exploratory relationships before she had qualified as a solicitor. And her feelings then had certainly been nothing like this!

It was a worrying reaction under the circumstances, and if there had been a way out of going to his house she would have taken it. She had a sneaky feeling that Hallam Lane would not leave her and Greg alone, even though he had promised.

On Friday Abby was in court; it was a trying and tiring day and she would have given anything to be able to spend the evening relaxing alone. She felt drained and washed out and not in the least like another confrontation.

Nevertheless, at five minutes to the appointed hour she halted her car outside the wrought-iron gates. A camera, which she had not noticed before, detected her presence and the gates were opened, presumably by Hallam Lane from inside the house. On her previous visit she had been compelled to announce her presence through an intercom system set into the wall next to the gates.

She drew her Rover to a halt in front of the magnificent red brick mansion that must have cost a fortune, and turned off the ignition. But before she could open the door Hallam Lane was doing it for her.

He had appeared out of nowhere and she looked at him in shocked surprise; then as she met the piercing blackness of his eyes Abby felt a further unexpected and unwanted jolt to her senses.

'You're on time. Good—I like that.' He was dressed casually this evening in a pale blue knitted silk shirt, open-necked and short-sleeved, with a pair of darker blue linen trousers. It was the first time Abby had seen him in anything other than dark colours and she thought how well the blue suited him. In fact he looked even more breathtaking than before and she knew it was going to be a difficult evening.

Abby herself had chosen to wear a chocolate-brown skirt and jacket with a cream blouse—very plain and very businesslike—her hair pinned on top of her head, no make-up at all on her face. She did not feel very comfortable; she never did when she wore such sombre clothes—they were so much against her nature—but she had not wanted Hallam Lane to get any more wrong ideas.

It was unfortunate that her skirt rode up over her knees as she climbed out and typical of Hallam Lane not to miss a thing. In fact his eyes stayed on her legs for far longer than was necessary, and when Abby bent inside to retrieve her briefcase she knew that he was studying her posterior.

His bold inspection sent her temperature soaring, and, as if in denial of the heated feelings that ran through her, Abby held her head that little bit higher as she accompanied him into the house.

He led her through to the same pleasant sitting-room that overlooked the expertly landscaped grounds at the back—and there was no sign of the younger Lane. She presumed he would be joining them shortly.

'A drink, Sommers?' he asked, indicating with a

movement of his hand that she should sit on one of the linen-covered armchairs near the French windows.

She shook her head. 'No, thanks.'

'Of course,' came the mocking response as he poured himself a generous measure of Scotch. 'I'd forgotten you were an abstainer.'

Abby doubted it; he struck her as the type of man who forgot nothing. 'Where's Greg?' she asked. She had no intention of sitting around wasting time when there was work to be done.

'He'll be joining us later.' Hallam Lane moved over to the white marble fireplace, where he rested his elbow on the mantelpiece and surveyed her indolently.

'Later?' Abby questioned with a frown, at the same time registering the way his close-fitting trousers hid none of the muscular strength of his thighs. He had to be the most potent male specimen she had ever seen, and it took her a second or two to drag her eyes back to his face and remember what they were talking about. 'What do you mean, later?' she questioned, her eyes sparking with irritation. 'Our appointment was for eight.'

'He's been detained.' There was curious pleasure in Hallam's voice as he made his announcement, and his dark eyes were watchful on hers, registering every change in her expression.

'I don't believe you.' Abby jumped up and crossed the room to face him. 'If Greg's not here then there's no point in my staying.'

A secret smile played about his generous lips. 'I thought we could spend a little while getting to—know each other,' he said softly, an innuendo in his tone that was distinctly disturbing.

'Then you thought wrong,' she retorted firmly. 'I have

much better things I could do with my time than make small talk with you.'

He took a slow sip of the amber liquid, watching her closely as he did so, an enigmatic expression narrowing his beautiful dark eyes. 'I'd like to talk about you. I'm curious as to why you chose law as a profession. With your looks and figure I would have thought you'd choose something more glamorous.'

Abby looked at him cool and hard. 'The answer's easy: I'm following in my father's footsteps.' When her parent had had a sudden and fatal heart attack a few years ago it had devastated her, her mother also, and they had consoled each other as best they could. Now her mother had a new boyfriend and she had her career and a place of her own. She was quite content.

'And you're happy without a man in your life?' There was a deliberate lift to his brows. 'Or is there someone? You see, I know so little about you.'

'My private life's private, and that's the way I'd like it to stay,' retorted Abby sharply. She had no intention of discussing her personal life with this man. 'I'm here to find out about your son, not for you to find out about me,' she told him. 'How long is he likely to be?'

Hallam Lane swallowed a further drop of whisky, savouring the smooth golden liquid to the full, before saying with what seemed like deliberate vagueness, 'I really have no idea.'

'No idea?' she countered, green eyes feverishly bright. 'This really is most irregular, Mr Lane. Is he upstairs? Can't you give him a call? I—'

'I'm afraid that's impossible,' he cut in quietly, his black eyes suddenly locked into hers, the suspicion of a smile curling his lips. 'Greg is not at home.' There was a certain amount of satisfaction in his voice.

Abby looked at him sharply and suspiciously. 'You didn't tell him about our appointment, did you? You deliberately let me come here, knowing that your son would be out.' Anger, fierce and swift, flooded her and she cursed herself for being so foolish. She should have known that she could not trust him.

Hallam Lane lifted his broad shoulders in acknowledgement, not in the least disconcerted. 'I can answer your questions myself.'

'You know exactly what happened on the night in question?' she asked, chin lifted, eyes blazing. Lord, what an idiot she had been.

'I know what my son told me.'

'Which need not necessarily be the whole truth,' she pointed out coolly.

Hallam Lane frowned. 'Why would he lie?'

'I'm not saying he's lied,' she retorted, 'but he could have quite easily held something back. Your son respects you, Mr Lane; I don't know whether you realise that. He wouldn't want to hurt you more than necessary.'

She recalled her younger brother—now married and living in the USA—getting into trouble on several occasions, but he'd never told his father every single detail, for the simple reason that he had not wanted to upset his father unduly—or incur further wrath!

Hallam shook his head, as though denying that this could be the case. 'I don't believe for one moment that my son would be so foolish.' And with an abrupt change of subject he added, 'I think it's time we ate.'

Abby stiffened, her finely shaped brows drawing together into a disbelieving frown.

'I did invite you for dinner,' he reminded her drily, a faint quirk to his lips.

'And I distinctly remember refusing,' she riposted.

'And since Greg is not at home then I see no point in staying.' She headed towards the door.

His voice stopped her. 'It's all ready; it would be uncivil of you to waste good food. And—there's always the chance that Greg will be back before we've finished,' he added softly.

He must have known that this would persuade her. She heaved a sigh and finally turned, to discover uneasily that he had moved away from the fireplace and was only a pace behind her. She drew in a deep, unsteady breath. 'I guess I am hungry,' she said reluctantly—actually she had eaten nothing since breakfast. 'But the instant we've finished—if Greg isn't here—I shall go.'

He smiled and, taking her elbow, led her out of the room. At his touch her stomach tied itself into knots, every pulse raced, and Abby wished that she had not been so quick to agree.

If Hallam Lane did not approve of her as his son's solicitor then why did he bother to entertain her? She wished she knew what thoughts were going through his mind, and she wished to goodness that she had spoken to Greg himself when he'd visited her office, so that this mix-up would not have happened.

The dining-room was next door, still overlooking the fine grounds. The rosewood table was laid with a cream damask cloth and cream napkins with a wine-coloured embroidered border. The candles were of the same deep red, as was the central single rose. There were two place settings only! Abby was furious. 'You had this arranged all along,' she declared, her voice shrill with accusation.

'What pretty girl doesn't like to be wined and dined?' he asked, a look of smug satisfaction on his handsome face—a look that told her everything was going according to plan—his plan!

She drew in a deep, unsteady breath. 'It looks set for a seduction scene to me, Mr Lane, and I can assure you I want no part of it. I refuse to sit here and eat with you and pretend that we like each other.'

'I'm not asking that you like me, Sommers.' There was a sudden crisp edge to his tone. 'I simply believe that it would be to our mutual advantage to spend a little time discussing my son.' A minute ago he had said he wanted to talk about her! 'That's an excuse and you know it,' she cried, her eyes flashing her hostility, and she turned to head out of the room.

Hallam Lane's fingers closed about her arm. 'You're not running out on me now,' he growled, twisting her round to face him.

'If you think that you can force me into staying you're making a big mistake,' Abby gritted, struggling in vain to free herself. 'I should have known you had an ulterior motive.'

'No, I haven't,' he told her firmly. 'And I have no intention of forcing you.' His black eyes met and held her luminous green ones. 'But there are certain events relating to my son's earlier years that I think are distinctly relevant to the trouble he's in now. I'd like to tell you about them.'

Again Abby was left with no choice. But why the devil couldn't he have told her all this in the office instead of using it as an excuse to entertain her in his own home? She eyed him warily, making it perfectly clear that she did not approve. 'Very well,' she said with a great show of reluctance.

'Good.' He let go her arm with a satisfied smile. 'Let me take your jacket.'

Unhappily Abby allowed him to slide it from her shoulders. She would have preferred to take it off herself but he had already made the move and she was compelled to endure the proximity of his hard-muscled body.

It shouldn't have disturbed her—she ought not to have allowed it to—but somehow it sent a tremor down her spine. And when he held out a chair for her his hands touched her shoulders; it was just a light brush, but nevertheless a further uneasy quiver ran through her.

Was this an omen of what was to come? Had she made a dangerous mistake? Ought she to get out now before anything further happened to upset her peace of mind?

CHAPTER THREE

FACING the window, Abby had an excellent view of the garden, but Hallam himself sat with his back to it, throwing his face into shadow. It put her at a definite disadvantage, she decided; it would have been much better if they had both sat sideways on to the window. Had he done it deliberately?

She looked beyond him. 'You have a nice garden, Mr Lane.' Mundane words, but she needed to say something—anything—to dispel her inner tension. She could accept that maybe he did want to talk about Greg but there had to be something more. Otherwise why the candles and the exquisite china? Why go to all this trouble?

It could be that he was trying to find out exactly what sort of a person she was. Perhaps he thought she expected this wine-and-roses treatment. Perhaps he thought all women expected it.

She recalled her unfortunate response to his kiss that first time he'd come to her office—could she have given him the wrong impression? Had he thought then that she was any man's for the taking? It was definitely a disquieting thought.

When she looked back at Hallam he was watching her, a faint, cynical smile playing about his lips. Abby had the troubled feeling that he was aware of every thought passing through her mind.

'Yes, I'm extremely pleased with the way the grounds

have developed,' he said. 'They're very different from when I first moved in, far less austere. We can take a walk afterwards if you like and I'll show you some of the changes I've had made.'

'I don't think so,' answered Abby coolly. 'I won't be here that long—unless, of course, Greg returns, though somehow I don't think he will. I think you've arranged this whole evening deliberately, though why I cannot imagine.'

A brow lifted but before he could make any response a woman's voice said, 'Are you ready for dinner now, Mr Lane?'

Abby gave a start of surprise. The door was behind her and she had not heard any footsteps.

'As ready as we'll ever be, Emily,' he answered pleasantly.

The woman came further into the room. 'You're Neville Sommers' daughter, aren't you?' she asked, peering at Abby closely. 'I thought it was you the other day but I couldn't be sure.' She was a thin, neat woman with short grey hair and a cheerful expression.

'That's right. Did you know him?' asked Abby.

'He looked after my late husband's affairs,' confessed the woman. 'You're very much like him, do you know that? There's no mistaking that you're father and daughter. I was sorry to hear he had passed away; he was very good to me.'

Abby gave a wistful smile, pleased to hear this woman's kind words. 'I miss him a lot.'

'And now you've stepped into his shoes,' said Emily briskly. 'Good for you, Miss Sommers. If you're anything like your father young Greg couldn't have chosen anyone better.'

Abby glanced at Hallam Lane out of the corner of her

eye. His lips were pursed disapprovingly. 'Food, Emily,' he said peremptorily. 'I'm starving.'

The woman immediately scuttled away and he looked at Abby curiously. 'I wasn't aware that Mrs Renfrew knew your father.'

'Does it make any difference?' she asked, sitting back in her chair and looking at him directly. 'Or is the issue still that you don't like to think I could be good at my job, especially as good as my father?'

'I know you're good,' he told her surprisingly, a quirk to his eyebrow as he spoke, 'or I would never have let Greg have his wish.'

'Meaning you've checked me out?' she asked sharply. It did not surprise her. Nothing this man did would ever surprise her.

His housekeeper chose that moment to return and he remained silent for a moment as the woman placed in front of them a delicious-looking fillet of Dover sole in a creamy white sauce with prawns.

'I'd have been a fool not to make a check,' he said once they were alone.

The smell of the food was profoundly appetising and Abby's empty stomach gave a loud rumble. She quickly took a mouthful and found the fish every bit as delicate and tasty as it looked.

'And yet you still don't want me defending your son,' she protested once she had emptied her mouth. Abby could not understand him. Hallam Lane was without a doubt the most enigmatic man she had ever met.

'I would have preferred a man.' Dark eyes looked challengingly into hers.

Abby flashed him a quick, indignant glance, wishing she could see him more clearly. Although the evening sun was not shining directly through the window the sky was extremely bright and his face very much in shadow. 'Is it women in general you don't approve of,' she asked, jabbing unnecessarily hard at her fish, 'or just women in what you see as men's jobs?'

He smiled slowly. 'Oh, I like women all right.' And his eyes dropped from her face to her breasts. His perusal, as always, was long and deliberate and induced a warmth in her skin that she could have done without. Abby wondered whether there was a hint here of what he had in mind for later, what he had perhaps had in mind all along—though she had been too dense to see it!

What a fool she was not to have heeded her earlier misgivings and left while she'd had the chance. She knew nothing about this man, had no idea what he was like—except that he was lethally attractive and equally dangerous. In fact he was the most threatening man she had ever met in her whole life.

Despite her misgivings Abby kept a tight hold on her emotions, letting none of her fears show. 'Do I presume from that that you have a lady-friend, Mr Lane?'

He dragged his eyes back to her face with a seeming effort. 'Hallam, please. And no, as a matter of fact there is no one special.'

'Why is that?'

His lips twisted with sudden bitterness. 'Let's say I tried it once.'

'Ah, your wife—she did this to you?' Abby knew she was out of order but the words spilled from her lips without conscious thought, and she was appalled to find herself adding, 'Actually, I don't blame her for leaving you; you're the most arrogant man I've ever met. No woman in her right mind would—'

'My wife is dead,' he cut in icily, stopping in an instant her angry flow of words.

Abby wished the floor would open and swallow her up. Hot colour flooded her cheeks and her whole body grew uncomfortable. 'I'm sorry. I—I didn't know.' Why on earth had she made the assumption that they were separated, that he was a divorced man and not a widower? Why hadn't Greg told her? Lord, how insensitive she had been. 'I really do apologise; I had no idea that—'

Again he interrupted. 'Let's drop the subject, shall we?' His eyes were ablaze with a light she could not read and for a few uneasy minutes silence reigned.

It was not until they had both finished their starter that Hallam spoke again. 'Do you live with your mother?' he asked, an agreeable, conversational tone to his voice now, as though the whole unfortunate episode had never taken place.

'No,' she said, shaking her head, at the same time breathing a sigh of relief. 'My mother has a new boyfriend; they're very much in love. And as I didn't want to spoil their pleasure in each other I bought myself a house.'

An eyebrow rose. 'No doubt out of the profits you make due to idiots like my son,' he remarked, a sudden bitter edge to his tone.

'Someone has to do the job,' she retorted, realising wearily that they would never see eye to eye. 'I can't understand you, Hallam Lane; why do you insist on making insulting remarks all the time?'

He gave an ironic twist to his lips. 'It's an amusing pastime.'

'Meaning you'll never take me seriously.' Abby's eyes flashed her displeasure. She always took umbrage when people were insulting about her chosen profession—and even more so with this detestable man!

'Meaning,' he said, 'that I would never even have given you the opportunity of taking Greg's case if he hadn't pleaded with me so eloquently.' He looked at her, as if trying to see her through his son's eyes. 'Goodness knows why.'

'Because he knows I'm good with young people his age,' she replied tartly.

His lips curled. 'Yes, I understand you've made quite a reputation for yourself. I have barrister friends who say that your groundwork is so thorough that you're a pleasure to work with. Why don't you have a boy-friend?'

His mercurial change of subject momentarily threw her and Abby looked at him with a frown before saying, 'As I told you once before, my private life is just that—private. It is none of your business.'

'Are you content to live the life of a nun?'

Even though she was deliberately staring out of the window Abby knew that Hallam was watching her closely and intently. To her dismay every nerve-end tingled. He had this alarming ability to arouse her just by looking at her, making her more aware of her own body than she had ever been before.

'You have no idea what sort of life I lead,' she told him sharply.

'So there is a boyfriend?' he insisted.

Abby could not lie and she shook her head. 'As a matter of fact, no, there isn't.'

'Does the job get in the way?'

She frowned. 'What do you mean?'

'Are men scared of you? Does being a legal eagle put them off?'

'Of course not,' she answered firmly, her eyes shooting sparks of indignation.

'When was the last time you dated?' He was sitting well back in his chair now, his head on one side as he deliberately studied her.

Abby felt a curl of desire in the pit of her stomach and stifled it instantly. 'Lord, what is this?' she cried, her tone more aggressive than she'd intended. 'The third degree? Of what possible interest can it be to you?'

He smiled. 'Let's say you intrigue me. I've never met a woman so uninterested in the opposite sex. Or is it, perhaps, all a sham?' he asked quietly. 'A veneer to go with the image of professional businesswoman?'

After a pause, when it became clear she was not going to answer his question, he went on, 'You did respond to me rather—easily the other day. I gained the impression that if I were to—'

His words were interrupted when his housekeeper returned with their main course, but the instant she left the room he continued, 'That if I were to make any further advances I wouldn't be exactly rebuffed.'

'Then you're deeply mistaken.' Fury made her raise her voice, and she hoped desperately that it was all presumption on his part, that he had not guessed what sensations crept through her body every time she looked at him.

Sliced breast of chicken, cooked in another one of Emily Renfrew's wonderful sauces wafted its mouthwatering smell beneath Abby's nostrils and she helped herself to vegetables from the dishes which matched the rest of the china, glad of something to do to take her attention away from Hallam Lane.

'Aren't we supposed to be discussing your son?' she asked in a deliberate attempt to change the subject.

He did not answer. Instead he asked a question of his own. 'Has anyone ever told you that your eyes are the most incredible green? So unusual. They change according to your mood. When you're angry they're as deep as a storm-tossed sea, but they're as light as the palest emerald when you're…'

He let his voice tail off, a knowing little smile playing about his lips.

Abby was appalled that he could read her so easily. 'You're despicable!' Her eyes flashed at him and she wondered what colour they were at that moment. She had no idea that they ever changed.

'I'm merely stating facts.' Amusement insisted on lurking at the corners of his mouth. 'Eat your food before it gets cold.'

Abby discovered that she had suddenly lost her appetite. Nevertheless she cut off a piece of chicken and put it into her mouth. Although it was undoubtedly tender it tasted like cardboard and when Hallam watched her every move she felt like throwing the whole contents of her plate into his face. In fact the thought gave her so much pleasure that she stifled a giggle, though she could not quite stop a smile forming on her lips.

'What's so funny?' he enquired as he also speared a portion of chicken.

'Private thoughts,' answered Abby, still smiling.

'I'll give you a penny for them.'

'You might not like what you hear.'

'Try me.'

She was sorely tempted—not to tell him but to carry the thought out. She could just imagine his reaction. She had done it to her brother once, when his tormenting had got the better of her. He hadn't been amused but it had been distinctly worth it just to see the shock on his face.

However, discretion had to be the better part of valour here. She shook her head. 'I don't think so.'

His mouth twisted, eyebrows rose and fell again. 'At least, whatever it was, it made you smile.'

Abby could see this being a long-drawn-out meal with the conversation centring almost entirely on herself, and she did not see why it should. 'I'm interested, Mr Lane—Hallam,' she said, in a further attempt to change the subject, 'in what line of business you're in. You have a very fine house here, well guarded; you give every appearance of considerable wealth. What do you do for a living?'

She had not truly expected that he would reply, had indeed expected an angry reaction. He seemed a very private type of man, more interested in asking questions than answering them. Nevertheless, to her surprise, he gave an indolent shrug and said, 'Nothing terribly exciting. I buy and sell precious stones; it's very mundane really.' He sounded totally uninterested in the subject, looking as though he would much rather be talking about her.

'You call that not exciting?' she exclaimed. 'It sounds wonderful. Do you travel the world?' Her eyes were suddenly alight with interest.

He inclined his head. 'Hence the need for security here while I'm away and Greg's at university.'

'Is Greg going to follow in your footsteps?'

Hallam's lips twisted wryly. 'It would make me happy if he did. Unfortunately he has shown no interest whatsoever.'

'Perhaps you don't involve him enough.'

'He reckons his studies take up all of his time.'

'What is his ambition?' At last they were on the subject of his son.

'He doesn't have one,' answered Hallam, his tone harsh all of a sudden. 'During his most formative years my son was brought up by my wife—if "brought up" is the right term. It is she who moulded his character.'

Abby frowned. 'I don't understand. Where were you?'

'We separated—several years before she died.' His tone was terse and suddenly bitter and a muscle jerked spasmodically in his jaw. 'And I blame her for the trouble he's in now.'

Trying to cope with the fact that he and his wife had split up after all, Abby said, 'For what it's worth, Hallam, I don't think he was involved. In fact I'm sure he wasn't. I believe everything he's told me. The other boys are simply using him as a scapegoat.'

Hallam snorted disbelievingly. 'Do you remember my telling you that Greg had been in trouble before?'

She nodded.

'It was while he lived with his mother. He stole from a local store. He was lucky that time; I doubt if he will be this.'

'I intend to do everything within my power to make sure he's not convicted,' she told him quietly.

His dark eyes locked with hers for several long seconds and Abby thought he was going to raise the question of his confidence in her yet again, but he didn't. He remained silent for a while, however, deep in his own thoughts, and then he shrugged his blackness off like a mantle and they began talking about other things.

He proved that he could be both entertaining and interesting, talking, after a little prodding from her, mostly about his work. 'My uncle gave me an uncut diamond when I was a young man—about Greg's age, I guess. I was totally fascinated by it and wanted to find out from where it came. It's how my career began.'

He went on to tell her about the Andamooka and Coober Pedy opal fields in Australia, the diamond mines in South Africa, what a thrill it had been for him when he'd first visited them, and when they took their coffee into the sitting-room she felt completely relaxed for the first time since meeting him.

Hallam swung wide the French windows. It was that breathless time between dusk and complete darkness. The odd bird still sang its sweet song and a honeysuckle growing outside the door wafted its heavy fragrance into the room.

Abby had said no to wine during their meal but when Hallam produced a bottle of Remy Martin and without even asking poured a generous measure into the bottom of a beautiful crystal glass, setting it down in front of her, she did not feel that she could refuse. She intended, though, to take only a minute sip at a time and let him think she was drinking the brandy when in reality she was doing nothing of the sort.

She had chosen her seat deliberately, suspecting that Hallam would join her if she sat on the two-seater couch. And such close proximity, feeling the heat of his body, smelling the musky maleness of him would undoubtedly be her undoing.

Unfortunately she had not counted on the fact that with him sitting directly opposite he was still able to watch her freely and, unfortunately, disturbingly. It was as bad as having him at her side.

Before pouring their drinks he had flicked a switch which put on several table lamps, but, when a couple of moths and various other flying insects found their way into the room, rather than closing the glass-paned doors Hallam turned the lights off again and they sat in the near-darkness.

Abby found this more than a little disconcerting. It was difficult to tell now whether Hallam was looking at her or not. 'I love this time of day, don't you?' she asked, surprised to hear a huskiness to her tone.

'It's my favourite. This and early morning. Are you a morning person, Abby?'

He had called her Abby. Not Sommers but Abby. She felt inordinately pleased. 'I guess I am,' she said. 'I like to go jogging or swimming first thing. It sets me up for the whole day. Do you exercise?' She could not believe they were having this sort of conversation, that he was actually being friendly. It was something she had thought would never happen.

'When I have the time I play squash,' he admitted, 'and I like swimming too.' He paused a moment, a sardonic lift of his brows. 'Just fancy—we have something in common.' But without waiting for a response he went on, 'In the main, however, I don't have the opportunity to exercise; it's my lifestyle that keeps me fit. I'm always on the go, always dashing here, there and everywhere.'

She wanted to ask whether this was the reason he had never found himself another woman, but somehow did not dare. She did not want to spoil the fragile rapport that was beginning to develop between them.

What had his wife been like? She had seen his disagreeable side; had that been the cause? Or was his wife the one who had been at fault?

'What are you thinking?' he asked. 'You look very serious. I'm sure they're worth far more than a penny this time.'

'Do you want the truth?'

'Naturally.'

Abby took a deep breath and decided to go for it. 'I was wondering about your wife.'

'What about her?' It was a harsh, guttural question, more a snarl than anything else, and Abby immediately knew it had been the wrong thing to say. Once again she ought to have kept her thoughts to herself. In fact it would have been better to tell him about throwing her plate of food all over him than this.

Nevertheless since she had started she might as well go on. 'I was wondering what she was like,' she said hesitantly, 'what happened to split your marriage up. I know it's none of my business, but—'

'You're damn right it's none of your business,' he ground out. 'But I'm glad you mentioned her because it's brought me to my senses. I was in grave danger of forgetting who you are and why you are here.'

What had she got to do with it? wondered Abby, but she knew she dared not ask any more questions. It seemed as though in some way he was connecting her with his wife, which was strange. Unless she looked something like her! Could that be it? Was that why he'd had it in for her right from the very beginning? Unfortunately there were no photographs in the room—otherwise she would most definitely have found some excuse to take a look.

Frowning now, Abby picked up her brandy glass, and unfortunately took a much longer swallow than she'd intended and choked as the burning liquid reached her throat. Tears came to her eyes and when her fit of coughing showed no sign of subsiding Hallam got up from his chair and began to pat her back.

His touch sent a tremor through each of her limbs, a tingling sensitivity to her nerve-endings. 'I'm better now, thank you,' she said, when she had taken about as much as her body could stand.

He had seated himself on the arm of her chair and she

could smell his subtle woody aftershave, which was both masculine and stimulating, but not overpowering—she could not even detect it unless he was close. He was certainly close now, too close for comfort, much too close—and when he made no attempt to move she pushed herself up. 'I think it's time I went.'

He stood also. 'Maybe it is,' he said gruffly.

'Could you get my jacket, please?'

As he went out he switched on the table lamps and Abby closed the French windows so that no more night insects would fly into the room. He returned before she had finished and she saw his reflection in the glass. For a brief moment she was able to study him, and to her dismay he appeared to be studying her also—and there was no mistaking the look of desire in his eyes!

Her heart did a double somersault within her breast but when she turned to face him she saw no more than a polite smile as he held out her jacket. She slid her arms into it, thinking that perhaps it had been her imagination—or even wishful thinking—until with a groan his arms slid around her waist and she was pulled hard back against his powerfully muscled chest.

It was all she had dreamt of ever since meeting him; it was what she wanted above anything else. Whether it had been his intention when he'd suggested she come to the house she did not know, and at this moment did not care. Her awareness of him had increased to such an extent over the last couple of hours that it was impossible to deny it.

'You're irresistible, Sommers,' he muttered thickly and surprisingly as he began to nuzzle the soft, delicate, infinitely sensitive area behind her ears.

His low voice brushed like velvet over her senses—a peculiar sensation Abby had never experienced before, causing her whole skin to rise in tiny goose-bumps. She found herself relaxing against him, sinking into that hard-boned body, inhaling the raw, exciting maleness of him. It was a heady sensation which threatened her sanity.

And when he spun her round to face him, his dark, sensual eyes locking into hers, it was as though a bottle of champagne had exploded in her stomach and all the bubbles were swimming along her bloodstream, bursting as they went, causing the most incredible sensations.

One hand began a slow caress over her back, the other cupped her head, and at the same time his lips sought and found hers. There was something excitingly different about being kissed by this man. He knew exactly what he was doing and what reaction it would draw from her.

His probing tongue teased her lips apart and Abby gave a tiny mew of satisfaction. No other man had ever kissed her so deeply or intimately, and she ought to hate it, considering the way he had treated her in the beginning. Instead she gave a shiver of pleasure, entwining her own tongue freely with his.

She was unaware of the exact moment he plucked the pins from her hair, conscious of it only when his two hands held her head close to his by her hair alone. There was something pagan and erotic about the action and in return she moved herself slowly and sensually against him. She wanted to feel the dynamism of his body; she wanted to experience this incredible pleasure that had been born out of nothing and was now enveloping her.

Their eyes were locked into each other's, desire and torture deep in both of them. It was not until, with a groan of desire, Hallam's hands slid down to her buttocks and pulled her hard against him that Abby realised it could all get out of hand. 'That's enough!' she cried.

But she had lost her chance to move. She was imprisoned by arms of steel, held hard against a body that was all pulsing manhood.

'How can it be enough?' he growled. 'How can I ever get enough of you?' His mouth continued to assault hers, his tongue to probe and explore and create further torrents of pleasure and desire. But then, so suddenly that she felt bereft, he let her go, muttering under his breath and shaking his head as if trying to divest himself of some unwanted emotion.

'That was unforgivable of me, Sommers.' His voice was thick and heavy and quite angry. 'It should never have happened. I think we both need some fresh air.'

'I think I should go,' she whispered. It would certainly be safe!

'No!' The word was said sharply and at the same time he took her arm and led the way outside to the vast landscaped gardens.

Abby wondered what force had suddenly taken hold of him, what had caused him to stop kissing her so suddenly—unless it was because he had remembered who she was. A career woman! One of the breed he so despised. He had had a lapse and was now angry with himself for briefly forgetting.

But if that was the case why had he insisted she walk with him now? Why couldn't he have let her go home? Why did he want anything else to do with her?

Although her head told her it was madness to get involved with this man, her heart told her differently. He was exciting, he was dangerous—he was adding spice to her sometimes humdrum life.

He walked a few feet away from her—deep in thought, eyes straight ahead. The garden nearest to the house was floodlit—the lights had come on automatically when they'd stepped outside—and Abby looked around her with avid interest.

Long, sweeping lawns led into a distance she could only imagine, and just out of sight of the house, beyond the terrace with its potted shrubs and colourful flowers, around the corner and behind a thick yew hedge, she discovered a kidney-shaped swimming pool. Lights beneath the water and strategically placed in the shrubs around it gave the whole area a magical air and Abby could not help exclaiming out loud.

'I didn't know you had a pool. Why didn't you tell me?' Her face was vibrant now, her eyes alight with pleasure as she took it all in; the classical marble statues standing on guard around it, the loungers, the white tables and chairs.

He was the first person she'd ever known who owned a swimming pool. How she would love to dive into those waters. 'Is it heated?' she asked eagerly. She knew that even in England's hottest summers and in the middle of the day the temperature of the water in outdoor pools was never great.

'Naturally,' he answered. 'Do you want to swim now?' He stood and observed with a wry smile the excitement on her face. She was unaware of the fact that she was hopping from foot to foot and looked nothing like a professional businesswoman, or indeed anywhere near her twenty-nine years, despite the severity of her clothes.

'Oh, I'd love to,' she said, and then added, 'If it wasn't so late and if I had my swimsuit with me.'

'Do you need one?' he asked darkly.

Abby felt swift colour warm her cheeks. 'Surely, Mr Lane, you're not suggesting that I go skinny-dipping?'

The very thought sent shivers across the surface of her skin.

'It did cross my mind.' He was looking at her in all seriousness now, though Abby felt certain that the thoughts inside his head must run along very similar lines to her own.

They had come out here to escape a difficult situation, not to subject themselves to something even more risky, more intense—more everything, in fact. Already her heartbeats were dangerously fast.

'It wouldn't be the first time I've done it,' he added softly.

With whom? Abby wondered. His son? By himself? A lady-friend? His wife? Dared she ask these questions? She did not like the thought that it could have been with another woman, lots of women. She preferred to picture him here alone, his long, lean, powerful body gliding through the water with effortless ease, muscles only faintly rippling, dark body hair hugging his skin like silk. Her mouth went dry at the very thought.

'I don't imagine it is,' she said at length. 'It's very private. Even if you had house guests you could still swim unobserved.'

'It's the way I like it,' he growled. 'So what is it to be? A swim, or shall we continue our walk?'

Abby swallowed hard. 'I think the walk.'

His lips curved into a cynical smile. 'Now why did I know that's what you would say?'

'It's what any girl with an ounce of pride would say,' she tossed over her shoulder as she began walking away from the tantalising blueness of the shimmering water, unaware that for a few moments he stood and watched her, observed with a tightening of his mouth the seductive, unconscious sway of her hips.

The grounds stretched endlessly, through parkland and woodland, alongside a swiftly flowing river, with only the light of a brilliant moon to illuminate the way. It also lit Hallam's face. Her own as well, presumably, she thought, but each time she looked across at him she saw how the moonlight accentuated the chiselled angles, making his eyes look like deep, dark, unfathomable pools—in which she could easily drown!

Their conversation was desultory, not about anything important, and Abby was glad because she needed all her concentration to make sure she did not fall. It was not really the sort of thing to do in high heels and more than once her heel sank into the soft ground, almost pitching her forward.

On each occasion a ready hand steadied her, but almost immediately he let her go again. It was obvious to Abby that Hallam had no intention now of forgetting exactly who she was. 'I think maybe it's time we went back,' she said, when she stumbled yet again.

'You're probably right,' he agreed gruffly. 'Otherwise you'll ruin your shoes and I'll be billed for those as well.'

Abby looked at him sharply, not sure whether he was serious or not, but it was too dark—now that the moon wasn't fully on his face—to see what his expression was, and so she said nothing, merely continued to wend her way back to the house.

Strangely, the silence between them was companionable, the odd bursts of conversation comfortable. She had thought there would be an atmosphere but there wasn't. She knew he had come out here to cool down his ardour—and apparently it had worked because there was nothing now in either his voice or his demeanour to suggest that he wanted to take her into his arms again and kiss her.

She wondered how angry he was with himself. On her own part her response to him had been a revelation. It had rocked her to the core. She had never experienced anything like it, and possibly never would again; she wouldn't be given the chance. He had most definitely had second thoughts and her guess was that after today she would never see him again—except in court, of course.

As they neared the house, as they reached the more decorative parts of the garden, the floodlights came on again. The house looked most impressive and Abby thought it was a pity that he lived here alone with his son. It needed a woman; it needed a family; it needed many children. Had that been his plan when he'd bought it? Had the breakdown of his marriage destroyed him? There was so much about Hallam that she did not know—and would never get the chance to find out.

They stopped again by the pool. 'Have you changed your mind?' he asked softly.

Abby was sorely tempted. The walk had done nothing to stop the torment that his kisses had induced; perhaps the coolness of the water would. Her whole body was still sensitised, still responded to his nearness. Even at this very moment she longed for nothing more than to be held in his arms again, to feel his lips on hers, to inhale the raw, exciting male scent of him.

She drew in a ragged breath. 'I don't think so.' It was sheer madness, every bit of it. The only sane thing to do was go home.

'But you'd like to, really, deep down inside?' His voice was suddenly much closer, much gruffer, more urgent; his hands were on her shoulders now, sliding her jacket off, dropping it onto a chair before twisting her in his arms to face him. 'There's only modesty stopping you, isn't there?'

'And common sense,' she cried in panic, when she realised that he was going to undo the buttons on her blouse and divest her of that as well. 'What on earth do you think you're doing, Hallam Lane?' Sanity had thankfully come to her rescue.

She swung away from him quickly but in her haste did not realise how close she was to the statue of Venus. She walked straight into it, twisted quickly away—and fell straight into the pool.

CHAPTER FOUR

ABBY felt stupid, a real idiot, and she surfaced to see Hallam taking off his shoes ready to dive in and save her. 'I'm all right,' she called, and started to laugh, the funny side of the situation getting to her. She had not quite anticipated swimming fully dressed.

But it didn't stop him; he dived in anyway. 'Are you sure?' he asked as he appeared at her side, a somewhat concerned expression on his face.

'Perfectly.' She grinned, dissolving into a further fit of giggles at the thought that he'd got his clothes wet as well—and entirely unnecessarily.

'Tell me you're not really a solicitor,' he said, shaking his head.

Abby knew that she didn't look like everyone's picture of a sombre, dark-suited individual; she didn't conform in any sense of the word. She grew suddenly grave. How could she expect him to take her seriously when she was behaving like a teenager?

'I'm sorry,' she said. 'It's just the incongruity of the situation.' And part of it was probably a hysterical sort of reaction. She desperately needed to get away from here, away from Hallam Lane and the torment he was putting her through, but how was she going to do it quickly now that she was soaking wet?

She hauled herself out of the pool, spurning his offer of help, and stood there dripping while Hallam did likewise. 'I guess it was my fault,' he said wryly, but she noticed he didn't really look sorry; in fact he looked as though he was trying to stifle a smile also. 'I'd better get you back into the house and dried off.'

Which could be a lengthy procedure, thought Abby anxiously, unless he had some clothes she could borrow. The thought of herself in one of Emily Renfrew's old-fashioned dresses induced a further fit of laughter—though this time she managed to keep it under control.

She picked up her jacket and looked around for her shoes—and realised they were still in the pool. Ruined, no doubt. They were new ones as well. Maybe she could put them on his bill! The thought brought a wry twist to her lips. He would not be amused.

Realising that her shoes were missing at the same time as she did, Hallam duly fished them out and carried them together with his own to the house. They entered through a side door which led along a stone-flagged passage to the kitchen.

His housekeeper threw up her hands in horror when she saw them. 'Lord, have mercy on me. What have you been doing?' It was obvious that she had never seen her employer in such a state before.

'Miss Sommers unfortunately fell into the pool,' he announced gravely.

'And you saved her?' There was adoration on the woman's face.

'I tried,' he said with wry humour, 'but this is one very independent young lady.'

And it seemed to Abby that he was grudgingly getting to like her, that his initial hostility was fading. She felt pleased, although she quickly assured herself that it was for Greg's sake. It would make handling his case so much easier.

'I'll take Miss Sommers upstairs so that she can get out of her wet clothes before she catches her death of cold,' he said. 'I'll pop them back down to you and perhaps you could…'

The older woman began to frown at the same time as she handed Abby a towel to mop her dripping hair. 'Perhaps I ought to see to Miss Sommers myself, sir.'

Abby could tell by his surprised expression that it was rare for his housekeeper to call him sir, and he clearly knew it meant that she found his suggestion unacceptable. But he nevertheless shook his head.

'That won't be necessary, Emily,' he said quietly, his tone suitably serious. 'You needn't fear that I intend to undress Miss Sommers myself—or even wait in the room while she disrobes. Everything will be perfectly respectable.'

Except that he had been more than willing to undress her outside, thought Abby, growing warm again at the very thought.

'Of course,' answered Emily, faint colour stealing into her cheeks. 'I didn't mean that, sir. I just thought I'd save you the trouble.'

He smiled and patted the woman's shoulder. 'You're a treasure, Emily.'

Climbing the stairs beside him, Abby was acutely conscious of their damp footprints, of their clothes dripping onto the deep-pile beige carpet and leaving little damp marks. He didn't seem to care, though, and when they reached the first-floor landing he opened one of the doors and took her into a beautiful large bedroom with antique furniture and floral wallpaper. 'The bathroom's through here,' he announced, opening an adjoining door. 'There's a robe behind the door. If you'd like to slip out of your wet things I'll—'

'When you've gone,' she announced firmly. Although he had convinced his housekeeper that his intentions were honourable she herself wasn't so sure. He had promised that he wouldn't stay in the room—and as far as she was concerned that meant the bedroom, whether she was behind the bathroom door or not. She was very vulnerable here and needed every assurance.

'Oh, come on, Sommers,' he said. 'This is no time to be coy.'

It was unfortunate that he chose that moment to graze his eyes over her wet blouse. She looked down and was horrified to see that the water had rendered the cream silk and bra beneath almost transparent. Her nipples were clearly visible, pushing hard against the wet material. His eyes seemed riveted to them.

'Get out!' she said, and it was all she could do to stop herself screaming. 'I'll leave my clothes outside the door when I've finished.'

His lips quirked; an eyebrow rose. 'Just remembered your position in life, Sommers?'

'I've realised what a swine you are,' she retorted. 'Stop goading me, for goodness' sake. The sooner I get out of these things and the sooner they're dry, the sooner I can go home. What do you think your son will say if he returns and finds me in one of your bedrooms?'

To her surprise Hallam smiled. 'He'll probably take it all in his stride.'

'Meaning that you frequently *entertain* the opposite sex?' she scorned, wondering at the stab of jealousy that pierced her heart at the thought.

His smile faded. 'Meaning nothing of the sort. You're jumping to conclusions, young lady. Isn't that something you're trained not to do?'

Abby could see the conversation getting them nowhere. She gave him one final glare and marched into the bathroom, relieved to find a lock on the door, snapping it smartly, and only then managing to relax.

Until she caught sight of herself in the mirrored wall. Lord, what a mess she looked with mascara streaked down her face, her hair in wet tangles, her blouse hiding none of the secrets of her body.

She could win a Miss Wet T-shirt competition hands down, she thought drily. How embarrassing it all was, how totally unethical. She was his son's solicitor, for goodness' sake. A pillar of society. How could he possibly treat her with any respect after this?

With an angry gesture she ripped off her blouse and skirt and bra and briefs, her suspender belt and stockings, and tugged on the white towelling robe. She held it round her for a few short seconds, her arms crossed over her body. She would remember this evening for the rest of her life.

But when an impatient rap came on the door and Hallam's loud 'Haven't you finished yet?' pierced her senses, she shook herself back to reality, picked up her wet clothes, and, opening the door, thrust them hard at him.

To her surprise he had already stripped off his own shirt and trousers and was wearing a robe also; it was cream with burgundy stripes, short and healthily male, revealing strong, well-muscled legs scattered with dark hairs—not too many, not too few. It was amazing how much she had taken in at one glance, she thought afterwards.

His room must be only next door, otherwise how could he have been so quick? Or was *this* his room? she thought in a moment's panic. But no, not with flowered wallpaper; it had to be a guest-room. It was neat and tidy with not a thing out of place. Certainly not in use at the moment.

His eyes alighted on her suspender belt which was unfortunately on top of the pile, and when an eyebrow quirked she wished that she had thought to wrap her clothes in a towel, out of the way of his prying eyes.

Most girls wore tights, she knew. Maybe he thought this had been deliberate. The fact of the matter was that she never wore tights—she thought stockings were healthier, and definitely more feminine. It was a lifelong habit.

'You'd best get showered,' he said gruffly, and Abby gained the alarming impression that he did not want to leave, that he wanted to stay here and... And what? It was a question she dared not contemplate.

The water was blissfully warm, like silk against her naked skin, the balm she needed to soothe her ragged nerves. She turned her face up to the gentle jets, eyes closed, letting it flow right over her for several long, luxurious minutes. Then she shampooed her hair and vigorously soaped her body, washed it all off and then climbed out. She towelled herself dry and was very tempted to slide into the comfortable-looking bed and curl herself up and go to sleep—until the door opened and Hallam Lane walked in.

Grateful that she had pulled the robe back on, and relieved that he was now fully clothed, Abby was nevertheless annoyed that he had entered without even a knock. 'Can't a girl have any privacy? It's all your fault this happened. If you hadn't...' Her voice tailed off. How could she say if he hadn't kissed her, when she had responded so readily? She was as much to blame as he was.

'Emily's put your clothes in the tumble-dryer,' he announced, ignoring her outburst, 'and there's a pot of tea waiting for us downstairs. It's her panacea for all ills,' he announced wryly.

'I'm to come down like this?' she asked sharply. Did he really think she would parade around his house dressed in nothing but a towelling robe?

His lips quirked. 'We could have tea here.'

'OK, I'll come,' she answered, trying to stem the quick panic that had risen inside her. 'I just have to brush my hair, that's all.' She returned to the bathroom where every conceivable style of brush and comb was laid out on a shelf. She chose a wide-toothed comb that seemed appropriate for her thick hair, but was compelled to take it into the bedroom because of the condensation on all the mirrors.

Hallam stood behind her, watching. She somehow expected him to offer to do it, was sure that he would and was glad when he didn't, but nevertheless she was acutely conscious of his presence and announced herself satisfied before she actually was.

'I've never met a girl with as many freckles as you,' he said suddenly.

His statement took Abby by surprise and she paused in the act of putting the comb down, her green eyes questioningly wide as she looked at him in the mirror.

'I've never thought they were particularly attractive either,' he added. 'Shows how wrong you can be. Let's go, shall we?' There was a sudden gruffness to his voice that suggested his mind was wandering onto other things, and Abby felt a soft warmth steal over her skin. She followed him quietly downstairs.

After her second cup of tea Abby wondered how long her clothes would be, whether she dared suggest going to ask. They hadn't spoken much and it was obvious to her that Hallam was keeping his feelings under iron control. It was understandable, she supposed, that his male hormones should wreak havoc since she was wearing nothing beneath the robe. Any man's mind would run amok. She wasn't happy with the situation herself.

And she was even more unhappy when she heard a door bang and Greg's cheerful voice calling out, 'Hello! Father, I'm back. Where are you?'

She glanced uncomfortably at Hallam, silently questioning whether it would be possible for her to escape before Greg saw her like this. But he shook his head and even as he did so the door burst open and his son erupted into the room.

He came to an abrupt halt, looked at his father, looked at Abby, and looked at his father again. It was easy to see what thoughts ran through his mind and Abby felt sure that her face had gone an unbecoming shade of scarlet.

Hallam, on the other hand, was totally relaxed. 'Abby fell into the pool,' he announced casually. 'Her clothes are drying.'

Greg smiled then, his tension easing. 'Really? Is that so?' And to Abby he added, 'I guess I should be sorry, but—' And to her surprise he began to laugh. 'I can't believe this. What are you doing here, anyway?'

Abby suddenly remembered how Hallam had tricked her. She sat up straight, her eyes flashing fire. 'It was supposed to be a business meeting. You were supposed to be here. Somehow, though, your father *conveniently* forgot to tell you. Excuse me—I'll go and find Emily. I'm sure my clothes are dry now.' And if she caused dissension between father and son she did not care. Hal-

lam Lane deserved it. He should not have done this to
her.

It made her feel better, laying all the blame on Hallam,
and after she'd collected her clothes and got dressed
again she presented herself in front of them both and
announced that she was leaving.

She sensed the tension between father and son and as
Hallam walked with her to the heavy oak entrance door
he said, 'That wasn't very clever, what you said to my
son.' He looked angry now and no one seeing him would
have guessed at the tender moments they had shared
earlier.

'It wasn't very clever, what you did to me,' she retorted. 'You deserve it. I hope he thinks the worst of
you. Tell him to come to my office first thing on Monday
morning—alone.'

Not surprisingly Abby had difficulty in sleeping that
night. Hallam Lane would not get out of her mind. His
kiss had triggered so many responses inside her that they
could not be dismissed lightly and she was glad that the
barrier was back up between them. It had been extremely
unwise to respond to him and she must make sure that
it never happened again.

Somehow she did not think it would. He was angry
with her now. She would be neatly categorised back into
her solicitor slot. She had Greg to deal with, however,
some explaining to do, and she hoped he did not feel
too badly let down.

Early the next morning, as was her custom on a Satur-
day, Abby went swimming with a group of girlfriends,
and she pushed herself to the limit of her endurance in
order to try and get Hallam Lane out of her system. She
was teased mercilessly, everyone wanting to know what

had given her so much energy, but the session did her good.

By the end of it she was back to her normal, happy, cheerful self and was able to think dispassionately about Hallam Lane. He was her client's father and had made a pass at her, but that was all. She felt confident it wouldn't happen again.

Nevertheless, as she prepared for work on Monday morning Abby hoped that he would not accompany his son. Her prayers were answered when Greg arrived punctually and alone, and she was able to breathe a sigh of relief.

'I'm sorry my father got you to our house under false pretences,' he said at once. 'I can't think why—unless he's interested in you. Do you think that's so?' He looked eager, as though he would be pleased if it was the case. 'It's been so long since he's shown any interest in another woman that—'

'Absolutely not,' she interrupted firmly. Any such thoughts had to be squashed firmly right now. 'He wanted to talk about you, that's all. He told me that you'd been in trouble before. Why haven't you told me?'

His cheeks coloured. 'I didn't think it really mattered. I was only twelve at the time,' he added painfully, 'and living with my mother. I was left a lot to my own devices. She had a new boyfriend.' His disparaging words said it all.

'I stole a computer game—purely to relieve my boredom, not because I hadn't got the money to buy one. When my mother asked where it had come from I couldn't lie and she made me take it back and apologise. The store fortunately took no action.'

'You were very lucky,' said Abby.

'I know,' he admitted ruefully. 'But it's the only time

I've ever stolen anything, honestly. It was a cry for help; I needed affection from my mother which I was not getting.'

'Your father mentioned that she is—no longer alive,' probed Abby gently.

Greg nodded sadly, a pained expression on his face. 'Yes—a road accident. Peter was driving—he was the boyfriend—they both died.'

'Do you miss her?'

'Of course I do.' He looked totally surprised by her question.

'Were your parents divorced?'

Greg shook his head. 'No, my father would never agree to it. He still loved her too much.'

'So why did they split up?' asked Abby, a puzzled frown scoring her brow.

'Because she was seeing another man,' he answered simply. 'Not Peter—someone else before him. They had some terrible rows about it and in the end she walked out. He fought tooth and nail for custody of me and was deeply upset when my mother won. He blames her for the trouble I'm in now.'

'Yes, I know,' she said quietly.

'But I wasn't involved,' he assured her. 'It had nothing to do with me. I've told you this before. I simply stopped to speak to Dean—he was their lookout—and when the police arrived I got dragged into it. You do believe me, don't you?' he asked earnestly.

Abby did, but he had no proof, no witnesses, and the rest of the gang were laying the blame on him.

'It won't be me who'll be doing the talking in court,' she informed him later. 'Harriet McDonald is the barrister who will be handling your case. She's very good. You'll meet her soon.'

'Another woman!' he declared, his gentle eyes widening. 'Father will be pleased.'

Abby was fully aware of that and had deliberately not told Hallam yet, but Harriet had an excellent reputation, as well as being a personal friend. They worked together a lot, and as a matter of fact Abby had arranged to see her the following evening.

It was one of the infrequent evenings they both had free and they'd planned to go out for a meal. Harriet looked frowningly at Abby when she came to pick her up. 'You look as though you've been overdoing it.'

Harriet was a thin forty-something, with short brown hair going grey, tortoiseshell spectacles which she more often than not waved around to emphasise a point, and a permanently cheerful expression. She had never married and had no intention of doing so. Most men were intimidated by her.

Abby did not dare tell her that the strain on her face was because of a man. She did not want to answer questions, nor did she want these troubling emotions. She did want to feel anything at all for Hallam Lane; she was quite happy with her life the way things were.

They ate at a quiet bistro on the outskirts of Shrewsbury and it was not until they got up to leave that Abby saw Hallam. Whether he had been there all evening or whether he had just come in she did not know, but he sat all alone in a secluded corner, and until he looked up and saw her he seemed to be entertaining some deeply disturbing thoughts of his own.

She gave him a tight-lipped smile as her eyes met his coolly impersonal ones; there was no warmth or pleasure in seeing her; no one would have guessed how passionately they had kissed only a few nights ago. She was therefore horrified to feel her whole body grow weak just by her looking at him, to feel the by now familiar warmth that stole through it, and she continued on her way out of the room without saying a word.

'Who was that?' asked Harriet once they were out in the car park.

Abby shrugged, trying to appear nonchalant. 'The father of young Greg Lane.'

Harriet looked very thoughtful. 'Mmm, looks like quite a man; you should have introduced us. Tell me something about him.'

'There's nothing to tell,' came back Abby's instant response. 'Hallam doesn't really want me to handle his son's case—he has something against career women. He's merely bowing to Greg's wishes.'

'So he won't be happy when he discovers that I'm involved too,' commented Harriet thoughtfully as she unlocked her car and they both slid inside. 'But I somehow sense more than you're telling me. You seem uptight. Are you sure that—?'

'I'm sure,' interjected Abby, her tone fierce. 'Now let's get going; I don't wish to discuss Hallam Lane further.'

When Harriet's car would not start she looked at her friend in dismay.

'It's going into the garage tomorrow,' Harriet told her ruefully, turning the key once again. 'It's been a rogue ever since I bought it.'

'I wish you'd said; we could have used mine,' said Abby. 'What are we going to do now?'

'Call the AA, I guess.' Harriet began tapping the Automobile Association's number into her mobile phone.

'Can I be of any help?' The driver's door swung open and the space was suddenly filled with Hallam Lane's huge frame.

Harriet shot Hallam a dazzling smile. 'Mr Lane, isn't it? Abby told me who you were. I'm Harriet McDonald. It's not often a knight in shining armour turns up at the right time. Perhaps you could give us a lift? My car seems to have died a sudden death, but as it's going into the garage tomorrow it's not worth tinkering with.'

Abby sucked in her breath; accepting assistance from this man was the last thing she wanted. The AA wouldn't have been long; they could have waited. What was Harriet playing at?

'It will be my pleasure,' he said with the broadest of smiles.

Ignoring Abby's *'Harriet!'* the other woman got out of the car and Abby had no option but to follow suit. 'I wish you hadn't done this,' she hissed as they hurried across the car park behind him.

Harriet grinned. 'You worry too much.'

The doors of Hallam's BMW were automatically unlocked as he pressed his remote control, and Abby slid quickly into the back. Harriet gave a questioning lift of her untidy brows and then joined her. But if Abby thought it was safer in the rear seat she was mistaken. Hallam's eyes met hers in his rear-view mirror and all hell let loose inside her.

None of the feelings from the other night had gone away. She had done her very best to banish them, to push them into a corner of her mind, but with just one look at him they returned with a vengeance. Her heart began to beat uncomfortably fast and she pressed herself back into the corner of the seat, where they could make no eye contact. It was imperative that she keep her feelings well hidden.

Harriet, with no such reservations where this man was concerned, chatted away to him happily in between giving directions to her house. 'Actually, I'm glad to have met you, Mr Lane,' she said cheerfully, 'since Abby's asked me to represent your son in court.'

The silence couldn't have been louder. Abby sank even further back into her seat and waited for the explosion.

He did not disappoint her. 'What the hell is going on, Sommers?' Hallam's voice, icily cold and accusing, was loud in the close confines of the car. 'You know my feelings on this score.'

'I don't think feelings should enter into it so long as people are good at their jobs,' she retorted evenly. 'Harriet is an excellent barrister; she rarely loses her cases.'

'Perhaps Sommers hasn't explained to you, Miss McDonald.' He turned his attention to the other woman. 'I do not approve of women doing men's jobs.'

'Yes, she's told me,' said Harriet agreeably. 'I think you're living in a past age, Mr Lane, if you don't mind my saying so. Ah, here we are—the white house just at the end. Thank you very much for the lift; you're more than kind.'

She jumped out as soon as he stopped the car, giving him no chance to say anything further, and she grinned infuriatingly at Abby as she said goodbye, knowing full well what a hornet's nest she had stirred up.

'Perhaps you'd like to sit in front?' he invited curtly.

Abby shook her head. 'No, thanks, it's not worth it since I only live a couple of miles away.'

'Yes, I know,' he said, much to her surprise. 'Atcham, I believe?'

Abby's head jerked. 'How do you know that?' And again their eyes met in the mirror. 'You have no right prying into my private life,' she protested, her spine stiffening with resentment. 'I can understand your checking up on me as far as my work goes, but anything else is simply not on.'

'When my son's name is at stake then, as far as I'm concerned, anything goes,' he said tightly. 'And I want you to find someone else to represent him; is that clear?'

'You'd be making a serious mistake if you didn't use Harriet.' Abby was fiercely protective of her friend. 'And I refuse to tell her that I've changed my mind. If it is your wish then *you* do it. Exactly what is it you've got against women in business?'

There was a tense pause before he spoke, and when he did his voice was thick with an emotion she could not understand. 'I have no intention of divulging my reasons to you.'

Abby could not understand him, but did it really matter? He could keep his reasons to himself so long as they didn't interfere with her work, so long as he let her and Harriet get on with their jobs.

Upon reaching the tiny village of Atcham, Abby was dismayed when he pulled up in front of her house without the need to ask for directions. It would appear that not only had he discovered her address but he had driven out here and found out exactly where the cottage was. The thought that he could have actually been sitting outside in his car while she was alone in the house sent further uneasy prickles down her spine. 'Have you been spying on me, Mr Lane?' she demanded, her tone fierce and aggressive.

'Not at all,' he answered easily.

Abby was not sure that she believed him, but knew that there was no point in pursuing the conversation. 'Thank you very much for the lift,' she said, and did not even look at him as she got out. It was not until she'd put the key in the door of her neat two-up two-down cottage that she realised he had followed. 'I can see my-self in,' she said clearly and loudly, desperately afraid that there might be a replay of Friday evening if she let him inside.

'One can never be too sure,' he answered, pushing the door wide once she had unlocked it, stepping into her tiny living-room and snapping on the light.

The place wasn't meant for people like Hallam Lane, for dynamic men with a powerful presence. He could have been five feet two and it would have made no dif-ference. It was his overall aura that counted. And he filled the room, totally dominated it—so much so that Abby found it difficult to breathe.

Nor did he look as though he wanted to leave. In fact he was glancing curiously around the room, as though it was important to him to see what sort of a place his son's solicitor lived in.

'Would you like a cup of coffee?' she asked, not re-ally wanting him to stay a second longer than necessary but feeling it would be churlish to kick him out when he had gone out of his way to help her and Harriet.

'Thank you. That would be very nice,' he said, so politely that Abby immediately felt suspicious. She un-happily closed the door.

Her stone-built cottage consisted of a living-room and kitchen downstairs, and a bedroom and bathroom on the first floor. Originally, when the house had been built almost two centuries ago, there had been two bedrooms, and the toilet had been outside, but the outbuilding had long since gone, and although losing a bedroom made the house small it was perfectly adequate for Abby's needs.

Until Hallam had walked in. Now it felt claustropho-bic, more especially when he followed her to the kitchen and lounged in the doorway as she put on the kettle. 'I hope you don't mind instant,' she said.

He shrugged. 'Whichever is easiest.'

And quickest! thought Abby, not liking the way his narrowed eyes were taking in every inch of her body. She had flung off her jacket as she'd walked through to the kitchen and now wished that she hadn't, because she was very well aware that her breasts had burgeoned beneath his steady scrutiny, her hardened nipples thrusting eagerly against the silky material of her blouse.

Giving him further proof that he had the ability to arouse her was the last thing she wanted and Abby was thankful of the opportunity to turn her back on him as she reached out for cups and saucers.

'It's a cosy little place you have here.' There was a rough edge to his voice that attacked her nerve-endings and increased her apprehension. 'But don't you ever get lonely?'

'Not really,' she answered, spooning coffee into the cups and still not looking at him.

'What do you mean, not *really?*'

Abby shrugged. 'I mean, no—I don't—ever. I have plenty of friends; I have hobbies; I don't have time to get lonely.'

'What sort of hobbies,' he asked, 'apart from swimming and jogging?'

A safe subject! She looked at him and smiled but it froze on her lips when she saw the blatant desire in his eyes. It was masked instantly but she had seen enough and a cold shiver of unease ran down her spine as she recalled what had happened when she had last seen such a look.

CHAPTER FIVE

ABBY slid her eyes back quickly to the cups, fiddled with the spoons in the saucers, the pulse at the base of her throat beating so wildly that it threatened to choke her. She had never been so thankful in her life to see a kettle boil.

'You haven't answered my question,' Hallam reminded her quietly. He still stood in the doorway. He hadn't moved an inch, and yet had managed to disturb her to such a degree that she hardly knew what she was doing.

'What's that?' she asked, wishing devoutly that she had never invited him to stay. It really had been a mistake. What she needed to do where this man was concerned was build a concrete wall ten feet deep around herself. And maybe even that would not keep him out. He would find some crack into which he could crawl and infiltrate her defences.

'I asked what keeps you occupied in your spare time,' he said, his voice a low growl that feathered the hairs on the back of her neck.

'Actually my interests are varied and numerous.' As Abby poured water into the cups she tried to inject some firmness into her voice. It would be fatal to let him see what a quivering wreck he was turning her into. 'But I suppose dancing is one of my favourites. Milk and sugar?'

'Just as it comes,' he answered. 'Shall I carry them through?' His voice was suddenly dangerously close to her ear and Abby felt a further devastating tremor run through each and every one of her limbs. It was all so much worse than she had expected.

'If you like.' She put the two cups on a tray and stood back while Hallam picked it up, anxious that they should not touch. There was not a lot of room in the kitchen and she would actually have much rather he'd got out of her way and left everything to her.

Her living-room was not very big either and it seemed even smaller once Hallam was seated in it. She drew the curtains and sank in a chair as far away from him as she could—which was no more than six feet—and all the time he watched her.

He had set the tray down on a low, well-polished oak table in the centre of the room and Abby felt inordinately grateful for the fact that it was between them. She had always felt that it was a cosy room, decorated in russets and pinks and greens, with traditional furniture and a few water colours painted by her father on the walls; now that cosy image had gone. Hallam Lane had instantly destroyed it. The sooner he drank his coffee and left, the happier she would be.

'What sort of dancing do you like?' His long legs were outstretched; he looked completely at home and relaxed—as though he was prepared to stay for a long time, she thought uneasily. His cup and saucer still sat on the tray, though she had picked up her own, finding it very necessary to have something with which to occupy her hands.

Abby shrugged. 'All sorts really, though I suppose Latin American is my real favourite. I love the square tango, and the paso doble. I used to belong to the local formation team. We won quite a few competitions.' And why was she encouraging conversation when the one thing she wanted was for him to drink his coffee quickly and go?

He nodded slowly, studying her with half-closed eyes. 'I can imagine you in one of those temperature-raising dresses; you have the perfect body for a dancer. You're so lithe and graceful that I knew immediately I met you that you had to do something like that. I must confess I find it much more difficult to see you as a solicitor. It's an odd combination.'

'Don't you have hobbies, Mr Lane?' she challenged coolly, feeling that he was still trying to put her down as far as her job was concerned.

'I guess I don't have a lot of time for them,' he said, a quirk to his full lips that told her he was still picturing her in one of her dance outfits.

'My hobbies and my job are two separate parts of my life,' she informed him haughtily. 'I need each of them. We all need some form of relaxation.'

'Do you have any brothers or sisters?'

It was a surprise question and she widened her eyes. 'A younger brother, yes. He's in America. He works for a major publishing company.'

Well-shaped brows rose. 'He didn't want to follow in his father's footsteps? Fancy that. It would have made a lot more sense.'

'You're a male chauvinist.' Abby's green eyes were unnaturally bright. 'I do as well as any man. My father was proud of me.'

'I've no doubt; you're a girl any father would be proud of,' he agreed. 'Intelligent, articulate, beautiful—but most definitely not solicitor material. How do you expect anyone to take you seriously looking as you do?'

'And how do I look, Mr Lane?' she challenged, every muscle tense as she glared at him. He was being insufferably rude tonight.

'Bewitching,' he growled. 'Tempting, captivating. Do I need to go on?'

Abby closed her eyes for a second. 'I think you should drink your coffee and go.'

'You do not like compliments?'

'Not when they come from someone like you,' she retorted. 'Someone who's prejudiced and narrow-minded and cannot accept that times change, that equality for women is now the norm. Tell me, do you eat often in Bryan's Bistro?'

He frowned, puzzled by her sudden change of subject, and drew his legs up, sitting straight now. 'Rarely,' he admitted.

'So why did you go there tonight?' Was it possible that he had seen her and Harriet enter that particular establishment? That he had followed them? That he had perhaps planned the evening to end this way right from the very beginning? Had he perhaps even tampered with her friend's car so that they would be compelled to accept his offer of a lift?

This latter thought was dismissed the moment it entered her head; Harriet had already said that the vehicle was playing up. But, even so, the coincidence of their meeting like this in a bistro she hardly ever used was strange, to say the least. Hallam Lane did not strike her as a man who would normally dine alone.

'Emily's gone to visit her brother in Exeter,' he answered, 'so rather than cook for myself I thought I'd eat out.'

It sounded a perfectly plausible excuse and yet Abby's doubt must have shown on her face because he added,

'You think that I deliberately followed you into Bryan's, is that it?'

Her guilty expression needed no words.

An angry frown darkened his brow. 'Good Lord, Sommers, why would I do that? If I'd known you were in there I wouldn't have ignored you. I was as surprised to see you when you stood up to leave as you obviously were to see me.'

'You have to admit it's a mighty big coincidence,' she pointed out. 'I don't go there very often myself—perhaps once a year, that's all.'

'Am I expected to apologise for intruding on your privacy?' he rasped, his anger deepening.

'You're intruding on it now,' she said pointedly.

He picked up his cup and locked his eyes with hers. It was unfortunate that he had such beautiful eyes, thought Abby. They did her heart no good at all. She took a much needed swallow of coffee to moisten her suddenly dry mouth. It was going to be impossible keeping this man out. Just sitting in the same room was arousing emotions that were difficult to subdue.

She wished desperately that he had kept things on a professional level right from the very beginning. Why had he felt it necessary to introduce personalities into their relationship? He must have known it would cause problems.

'Something tells me,' he said, dark eyes still closely watching her, 'that the reason you don't want me here is because you're finding it difficult to control your feelings.'

Abby frowned, appalled that he could read her so easily. 'What nonsense,' she countered heatedly. 'What typical male conceit. I'm tired, that's all, and I have a busy day tomorrow.'

Hallam glanced at his watch. 'It's a little after ten, not really late. I think you're lying.' His lips quirked as he spoke.

'Why should I do that?'

He smiled then—a faint smile, but a confident one all the same. 'To protect yourself. You'd need to be inhuman not to feel something after Friday night.'

'You're under the impression that meant something to me?' she asked caustically. 'All it did was prove that harassment comes in all forms.'

'You think that's what it was?'

'What else?' she flashed. 'You were obviously trying to prove that I'm not a competent solicitor, not a complete professional. Maybe I should make it quite clear right here and now that that is not how I normally behave. I have no idea what came over me but you can rest assured there'll be no recurrence. And you most certainly won't get me to your house again under false pretences.'

He inclined his head to one side and looked at her darkly. 'I felt the need to talk to you, Sommers, in order to find out all I could about the woman my son praises so highly.' His lips quirked. 'As it happens, I found out quite a lot.'

'Damn you!' she said angrily. 'I think you're trying to belittle me, perhaps even to make out that my ethics are not good enough for the job I do. I think that is why you kissed me. I think you'd use any means to get me off Greg's case.'

She was on her high horse now, green eyes shooting sparks of annoyance, her whole body tense. 'But you won't win,' she continued strongly. 'You won't drag me down to your level. My job means everything to me; I will not have you undermining it.'

Black brows rose reprovingly. 'It is not my intention to establish that you're incapable,' he said. 'Time alone will tell me that. But you are without a doubt a most beautiful woman—far too distracting for a man's peace of mind.'

Abby looked at him uneasily. 'I don't flaunt my sexuality, Mr Lane, if that's what you're insinuating. And I don't think this is the sort of conversation we should be having.' She pushed herself to her feet. 'I'd like you to leave.'

He hauled himself up but, to her intense astonishment, instead of moving away from the table and towards the door he came to her, and stood so close that there was no avoiding him. His unfathomable eyes locked into hers.

I could get drunk on just the smell of this man, she thought painfully. He was totally overpowering, the most masculine male animal she had ever met. And she wished he would go. He was arousing emotions she would have far rather not thought about.

To her intense dismay he lifted a hand to touch her flaming red hair as it framed her face and fell over her shoulders in an abundance of thick waves. He seemed mesmerised by it. Then his fingertips lightly touched the sides of her face—a feather-light caress which triggered an electric response. It was madness allowing it but for a few heart-stopping moments Abby was unable to move. She felt hypnotised, totally under his spell.

She was both surprised and relieved when his face tightened, when a dark, savage flush stole across his features and he dropped his hand smartly to his side. 'I guess it *is* time I went,' he said gruffly.

Neither spoke as she opened the door and let him out, and she closed it again softly behind him, standing a moment against it, waiting for him to start up his car and leave. And only then, when she knew he was safely out of the way, did she gather up their cups and take them through to the kitchen.

She really did wish that Hallam hadn't touched her; she was positive that she had given him no encouragement, other than stand drinking in the male scent of him for a couple of seconds.

It was a bewildering situation that she found herself in, and sleep that night proved almost impossible. Dawn was breaking when she did finally manage to drop off, and when her alarm sounded at seven-thirty she felt like a zombie as she went about her normal routine.

As the day wore on she felt better but at the back of her mind Hallam Lane still niggled. Harriet predictably telephoned and wanted to know what had happened after they'd dropped her off the previous evening. 'I guess I let the cat out of the bag before you were ready,' she said mischievously.

'He wanted me to tell you that you couldn't represent Greg,' Abby told her.

'Did he now?' mused Harriet. 'What did you say to him?'

'That he had to do his dirty work himself.'

Harriet laughed. 'He's quite a gentleman actually. And do you know what I think? That he's interested in you. I might be wrong, but I think this is where the problem lies. He's declared he doesn't like career women and now can't see a way out of it. It's why he's angry all the time.'

'You're totally wrong,' said Abby fiercely. 'That's a totally ludicrous suggestion and you know it. Hallam Lane has no more interest in me than I have in him. And when the case is over I don't expect, or ever want, to see him again.'

Week followed week and the court case drew nearer and, much to Abby's relief, Hallam Lane kept out of her life. She and Greg had a long talk with Harriet, and the barrister seemed very confident that they would win.

Sleep became easier, although there were still occasions, perhaps too frequent for her peace of mind, when she recollected the excitement of his kisses and wished that they had met under different circumstances.

On the day of Greg's case Abby dressed in a severe navy suit and pale blue blouse, her Titian hair pinned up, her navy blue shoes moderately heeled. She applied her make-up carefully so that it almost looked as though she wasn't wearing any, and finished with a pair of pearl earrings.

She knew that today she would see Hallam again and the thought was already causing a much stronger adrenaline flow than she'd expected, or wanted, or needed! Although Harriet would be doing all the talking it was imperative that she keep her wits about her—and how could she do that while feeling such a strong sexual awareness of her client's father?

It was an unfamiliar scenario. Always in court her mind was razor-sharp—and it must be today, she told herself firmly. She must not let this obsession with Hallam Lane lessen her concentration.

Obsession! Abby was horrified that such a word had even occurred to her. She wasn't obsessed with him, was she? She found him faintly attractive but that was all. She hadn't even thought about him for weeks—well, not much anyway, she tried to convince herself. And he was certainly not going to disturb her today.

Why then, she asked herself later that morning when

she met Greg and his father in the court building, did her heart run amok? She was careful not to let it show, careful to maintain a dignified image, shaking both men's hands as the formality of the situation dictated.

Greg was clearly nervous, his gentle face pale, his hands twisting unduly. Hallam, on the other hand, showed none of his emotions. He was, as always, in complete control of himself, and although he looked closely at Abby he too was suitably grave.

Harriet came rushing into the waiting room a few minutes later, took one look at the serious trio and burst into laughter. 'Lighten up; we're going to win this case,' she said. 'Have no fear about that.'

It was not only about the case, thought Abby; it was about emotions. It was the tension between her and Hallam—although whether he felt it too was a different matter. Maybe he *was* solely concerned about Greg—he had aired his doubts about her ability to build up a strong enough defence very vociferously indeed.

Finally it was their turn. The hearing was short, Harriet brilliant, and Greg found not guilty. There were wide smiles all around. Hallam shook the barrister's hand and thanked her, and did the same with Abby. But Greg embraced her warmly and joyfully. 'Dad and I are going out for a celebratory lunch—he already promised if I got off. Will you join us?' His eyes were shining as he looked at her.

About to refuse, Abby perversely changed her mind when she saw Hallam's frown of disapproval. It would be interesting to see exactly what his attitude towards her was now that his son had been cleared, now that she was no longer a necessary part of their lives.

Abby thought she knew. It would be, Thank you very much and goodbye, Sommers. No more kisses, no more nothing, but it would be interesting to see how he handled it. She smiled broadly. 'Yes, Greg, I'd like that. Thank you. Is Harriet included too?'

But before he could answer Harriet shook her head. 'Count me out; I'm too busy.' And in an aside to Abby she added, 'Now that's out of the way perhaps you and Hallam will get together. Good luck.'

'I don't need luck,' emphasised Abby quietly. 'I shall be glad he's out of my life.'

'Then why accept the luncheon invitation?'

'To please Greg.'

Harriet's expression suggested that she believed no such thing and she gave Abby a knowing smile before hurrying away in the direction of the car park.

'You'd best come with us,' said Hallam curtly.

Thanks for making me feel welcome, thought Abby, and almost wished that she hadn't been so eager to accept Greg's invitation. 'I'll follow in my own car, thank you,' she replied, equally coolly.

He lifted his broad shoulders in an indifferent shrug. 'If that is your wish.'

'It makes sense,' she retorted. Otherwise she would have to rely on him for a lift back or take a taxi, and what was the point?

Greg looked worriedly from one to the other, sensing the antagonism and obviously wondering whether he had done the right thing. She guessed it had been a spur-of-the-moment invitation and now he was probably wishing he had not asked her.

Abby immediately felt sorry for him. He had gone through a lot these last few months and needed no further upset. She gave him a warm, reassuring smile. 'What are we waiting for? Let's get going.'

There was an expression on Greg's face that suggested

he would like to ride with her, but when his father barked, 'Greg!' he turned quickly and got into the BMW.

Hallam drove at speed from the courts and because Abby had not thought to ask where they were eating she was compelled to keep up. Finally, on the outskirts of Shifnal, they arrived at a huge old manor house that had been turned into a hotel and restaurant.

It had an air of old-fashioned grandeur and Abby liked it immediately. The service was quietly discreet and very efficient and as they sipped their pre-lunch drinks— Abby had ordered only mineral water—she let her eyes wander around the high-ceilinged room.

'I'm glad to say my distrust in you wasn't justified, Sommers.'

Her attention was brought swiftly back to her companions. 'Is that a compliment?' she asked coolly, allowing her green eyes to widen with faint scorn as she looked at Hallam Lane.

'I guess it is. It's a thank-you for clearing my son's name.'

It sounded a very grudging acknowledgement of her and Harriet's success, thought Abby. It would have been better had he said nothing. 'I only did what I'm getting paid for,' she answered tersely.

'Of course.' It was a dry response, and his dark eyes were unreadable.

'I for one am extremely grateful to you,' chipped in Greg urgently. 'You and Miss McDonald.'

She turned a winning smile in his direction. 'Thank you, Greg. It's very kind of you to say so.'

'You can't imagine how worried I've been. The odds seemed all stacked against me. I never truly thought I stood a chance.'

'I knew you were innocent,' she said quietly.

'I appreciate your faith in me.'

'Enough of this mutual admiration society,' growled Hallam. 'Finish your drinks; our table's ready.'

The whole meal was soured by Hallam's less than friendly attitude but at least she now knew where she stood. There would be no more kisses, no more late-night coffees. This was the last she would see of Hallam Lane.

In one way she was disappointed, in another relieved. It would save her the heartache because she would never have known where she stood with this man. Her ears suddenly picked up on what Greg was saying to his father.

'I think she would enjoy it very much. It is the least we can do for her, considering how hard she has worked on my behalf. Please, Father.'

Abby's eyes met Greg's and then Hallam's and she wished she knew what they were talking about. The young man looked eager and excited, his parent less so. In fact Hallam's lips were clamped into a tight line and it was perfectly obvious that whatever his son had asked of him did not meet with his approval.

'I am sure that Miss Sommers is far too busy.' His dark eyes pierced Abby's with such intensity that she almost felt a physical pain. 'Isn't that so?'

'If I knew what you were talking about I might be able to answer,' she retorted, holding his gaze with difficulty.

'Greg has just suggested that you accompany us to France,' he remarked tonelessly.

'France?' she echoed, her eyes widening as she looked from Hallam to his son.

'Yes. We have a villa there,' explained the younger

man. 'We're going on holiday for the rest of my summer vacation. I'd like you to come,' he added sheepishly.

'But why?' A holiday in France! With Hallam! Forget Greg! Her whole body pulsed now, a deep, prickling heat making her feel uncomfortable.

'Because you'd—'

'Greg!' cut in his father sharply. 'Let Miss Sommers speak for herself.' He looked at Abby. 'The choice is yours.' He clearly did not expect her to accept, and he clearly did not approve of his son's inviting her—though he was too polite to say so in front of Greg.

Wait until they were alone, she thought; he would certainly have something to say to his offspring then. 'When are you going?'

Hallam's eyes narrowed slightly at her question. He had evidently expected a straightforward no. 'Tomorrow.' It was said with great satisfaction.

Abby felt acute disappointment. There was no way she could reorganise her workload so quickly, if she did say yes—and Lord, how she wanted to. It was her heart ruling her head, she knew that, but in truth she was dreadfully in need of a holiday.

'You could come out to us,' insisted Greg, seeing the shadow on her face.

It would be highly dangerous, she knew, because Hallam had crept beneath her skin to such an extent that even if he didn't speak to her for the whole time she was there it would not matter. Just being with him would be excitement enough.

And torment, she reminded herself. She was a fool even to consider it. But Greg would be there. Hallam could not possibly do anything with his son around. She would be safe. But did she want to be safe? Wasn't her physical need of this man the very reason she wanted to go? Wasn't it the only factor?

'Well, Sommers, we're waiting.' Hallam's deep voice burrowed into her thoughts.

She looked at him with a faint smile, anticipating the shock when she gave him her answer. 'Actually I think I might like it. I am due a holiday, although, of course, I couldn't leave tomorrow; there's too much I have to sort out.'

His face froze, eyes so icy that they chilled her. She had not expected this. She had expected some adverse reaction, but certainly nothing so strong. Abby shivered and wondered whether she ought to retract her words.

But Greg was already speaking. 'That's wonderful; I'm so pleased. She'll love our villa, won't she, Father? It's right on the edge of the ocean and—'

'That's enough, Greg,' thundered Hallam, and even his son looked amazed at the ferocity of his tone. Then he said to Abby, 'I'll let you have the telephone number of the villa so that you can let me know when you're ready to leave. My private jet will fly you out.'

'Private jet?' Abby's mouth fell open stupidly.

He ignored her comment. 'And now, if you've finished, we'll go. I also have things to do before we leave.'

On her way back to the office Abby doubted her sanity. She could not believe that she had just agreed to spend time in France with a man who had no time for her. She had made the wrong decision; she must not go, even if it meant hurting Greg in the process. It would be a fatal mistake.

For the rest of the day Abby found if difficult to concentrate and it was a relief to get home. Stripping off her suit and blouse, she wrapped herself in a silk kimono, flung herself onto the settee and closed her eyes.

Her mind was a kaleidoscope, all the day's events mixed together in colourful, confusing patterns. And then the doorbell rang.

Her heart slammed against her ribcage and she hoped to goodness it wasn't Hallam, or Greg come to say how pleased he was that she had agreed to join them.

It was neither. It was Harriet, wanting to know how lunch had gone.

'Dreadful,' groaned Abby. 'I made the biggest mistake of my life. Come in and sit down; there's a pot of coffee on the go if you'd like one.'

'You've got a date with Hallam?' suggested her barrister friend, sounding delighted, declining the offer of a drink, perching instead on the arm of a chair.

'Worse than that. I've agreed to go on holiday with him.'

Harriet gave a hoot of laughter. 'Goodness, you certainly don't do thing by halves. This is unbelievable. How——?'

'But I'm not going,' interrupted Abby strongly. 'I'm deranged; I have to be. How could I have agreed to such an insane suggestion?'

'Now wait a minute,' said Harriet. 'You need a holiday; you know you do. You haven't had a proper one for years.'

'Maybe.' Abby shrugged. 'But a holiday with Hallam Lane? I ask you. It's the last thing I want.'

'Then why did you agree?'

'His son invited me,' she answered reluctantly, 'and it seemed like a good idea at the time.'

'Why?'

Abby laughed. 'Goodness, Harriet, I'm not in the witness box.'

'But you must have had a reason for saying yes. It's

not like you to be impulsive; you always think things through carefully. You're in love with the guy, aren't you?'

In love! With Hallam Lane? What a ridiculous idea. 'Of course I'm not,' she retorted.

'I think you are,' said Harriet. 'Take a good look at yourself, Abby. I've never seen you in such a state over any man.'

'I'm not in a state,' Abby insisted.

'No?' Harriet's eyebrows rose sceptically.

'No!' she repeated firmly.

'I know what I see.'

'And I know what I feel.'

Harriet eyed her friend sternly. 'And exactly what is that?'

'I don't love Hallam Lane. How could I love such a chauvinistic pig? I hate him.'

Harriet took off her glasses and waved them expressively in the air. 'Strong words, my friend. Too strong in fact. You know what they say about people who protest too much.'

'I *don't* love Hallam,' insisted Abby. But she did feel something!

Harriet smiled—a secret, knowing smile. 'Maybe not now but you're very close to it, and if you don't go on that holiday you'll always regret it. It's an opportunity to find out exactly what your feelings for this man are. You'll have a chaperon in Greg anyway, so what are you worrying about? Take the chance, girl, and go.'

CHAPTER SIX

LONG after Harriet had gone home Abby sat thinking about what her friend had said. Could it really be love that she felt for Hallam Lane? Not a strong chemical attraction but love? And *if* it was—a very big if—then wouldn't spending a holiday with him be the very worst thing she could do? Wouldn't she give herself away? Wouldn't she make a fool of herself?

Why had Greg asked in the first place? she mused. And what on earth had prompted her to accept? It was the very last thing she should have done. It was crazy, it was stupid, it was illogical—and she had never done anything illogical in her life. Maybe it was love that was addling her brain. It was making her act completely out of character.

But no, she refused to accept that it was love. How could she love a man who had made it perfectly clear that whatever little bit of interest he had shown in her was only for the sake of his son? He had been cultivating her, that was all—using her, making sure she would do her best for Greg. And now that the case was won his attitude towards her had completely changed. He did not want her joining them on holiday; he had made that perfectly clear. He did not want to see her ever again.

It was impossible to sleep after that, and impossible to concentrate at the office the next day. She left early and had just got home when the telephone rang. 'It's me, Greg,' came the eager voice. 'I'm just checking to make sure you haven't changed your mind. I really want you to come, Abby. I can call you Abby, can't I? I know my father calls you Miss Sommers, or Sommers even, but you're nearer my age and—'

'Greg, Greg!' Abby managed to get in a word. 'Of course I haven't changed my mind.' Now why had she said that after all the hard thinking she had done, after the decision she had made?

'So when will you be coming?' he asked quickly.

'I can't tell you that just yet,' she answered. 'There's so much I have to do at the office.'

'I think you won't come.' He sounded suddenly despondent.

'I've said I will, haven't I?'

'But people don't always keep their word.'

'I will,' she said firmly, wondering why he was being so insistent.

'You will?' He was eager again instantly.

'Yes, Greg.' And now there was no backing out. She was making a big mistake, she knew that, but she could not bear to hurt Greg. At least, that was the excuse she kept giving herself.

It was easier than she'd thought to rearrange her diary. Grypton and Evans were all for her taking a break, said it was long overdue, and fortunately she had no court appearances after Friday for three whole weeks.

Therefore, one week after her luncheon with Hallam and Greg she found herself dialling the telephone number of their villa. Her heart raced at the thought that Hallam himself might answer; she had thought about nothing but him ever since she had agreed to go. He had disturbed her thoughts; he had disturbed her dreams; he had disturbed her, full stop. There were times when she had thought about forgetting the whole thing, and others when she could not wait to get there.

But when she heard a soft female voice on the other end of the line—a husky, extremely sexy voice—Abby once again questioned the wisdom of what she was doing. He had a woman friend!

Was that why Greg had been so insistent—he felt left out with his father spending all his time with his French girlfriend? But then she recalled Greg saying that his father had never shown any interest in other women. So was this a new girlfriend? There were so many unanswered questions.

'*Qui est à l'appareil?*'

'Er—Abby Sommers,' she answered reluctantly.

Surprisingly the girl seemed to know who she was. '*Mais oui!* Hallam, he is expecting you.' Though, judging by the tone of her voice, she herself was not happy about it. 'One moment, please; I will fetch him.'

Abby had the perfect opportunity to terminate the call but even while she was deliberating Hallam Lane's harsh voice sounded in her ear. 'Sommers?'

'Yes.' Her response came out almost as a squeak. If she had expected a welcome she certainly wasn't getting it.

'You're ready?'

This was her last opportunity to change her mind and she thought hard for a few seconds before finally closing her eyes, taking a deep breath, and saying, 'Yes, I'm ready.' And she wasn't sure whether it was Greg or her own puzzling emotions that had made the decision for her. Greg needed her, that much she knew, but did she need the heartache and unhappiness that would inevitably follow?

'Then my plane will be waiting at Shawbury airport at eight-thirty in the morning. Be there.'

He put the phone down before she could speak again, and so it was done, it was arranged, there was nothing else she could do about it. But the thought persisted that there would be another woman present. She would be compelled to watch Hallam and the French girl together.

Jealousy was surprisingly rearing its ugly head. She had spent the last week convincing herself that she did not love Hallam; now she felt totally confused. If she didn't love him then why the green-eyed monster now? She ought to have put the phone down immediately a female voice answered; it would have been best all round.

She could still back out, thought Abby the next morning as she got ready. It wasn't too late; all it needed was for her not to turn up at the airfield—but curiosity motivated her. She wanted to see for herself what type of woman Hallam preferred, even if it meant stabbing a knife in her own back in the process.

Nevertheless, perhaps she would still be able to enjoy a relaxing holiday, she decided—soak up some sun and do absolutely nothing. But she added wryly as she snapped the final lock on her suitcase, Who am I trying to kid? Relax was something she definitely wouldn't do, not if she had to sit and watch Hallam Lane with someone else.

Believing that what she felt for Hallam was nothing more than physical had made her feel relatively safe. It had been the sort of thing you could walk away from without getting hurt. Now the gremlins were eating away at her insides and she did not know what she felt any more. Could it really be love? And if so how had it happened? And what was she going to do about it?

She heaved her case into her car, locked the house, and set off. She had plenty of time. Having hardly slept a wink all night, she had been up at the crack of dawn, drinking gallons of coffee but unable to face the thought of food.

At eight precisely she reached the small airfield which was not many miles from her home. A plane sat on the runway and as she ran her car into the parking area a young man marched towards her. 'Abby Sommers?'

She nodded, a little surprised. She had expected to sit around waiting for the next twenty minutes or so.

'Your plane is waiting. Let me help you with your luggage.'

In the space of a few seconds she had crossed the tarmac and was climbing up into the aircraft. When she saw Hallam Lane sitting behind the pilot she gave a gasp. 'I didn't expect you, Hallam,' she said. 'You didn't have to take time out of your holiday.'

There was an expression in his eyes that she could not fathom, a sort of gleam of anticipation—or was it displeasure? It was gone instantly, replaced by a bland look that told her nothing.

'Since I have,' he replied, 'you might as well relax and enjoy it.'

Relax! Enjoy herself! There was not much chance of that with her heart pounding at three times its normal rate. No matter that she had warned herself sternly to keep her feelings in check. Everything jumped into vibrant life just by her looking at him, and when she settled herself beside him it was even worse.

She could smell the familiar, exciting maleness of him, feel the warmth of him, experience a mind-shattering awareness of him. It did not bode well for the next two weeks and if she could have scrambled off there and then she would have done.

But the pilot had clearance and was already taxiing along the runway, slowly at first and then with increasing speed until they soared like an eagle. It was too late now to do anything about it. She had burned her bridges, as the saying went. She was committed. She was spending the next two weeks in Hallam Lane's villa whether she liked it or not.

More used to 757s than small jets like this, Abby felt distinctly nervous. At least, she tried to convince herself that it was the plane and not Hallam who was tightening her muscles and curling her fingers into fists. She didn't really succeed.

'Is Greg enjoying his holiday?' she asked, actually wanting to know about the other girl he had cosily installed in his villa.

'I believe so,' he answered, 'though he does seem to get bored easily. Actually he doesn't often come to France with me; I think he would much prefer a holiday with his friends. He's looking forward to you joining us.'

But you're not, she returned silently. It was there in the set of his shoulders. He was as tense as she was. She wondered whether Hallam had insisted Greg join him this time, possibly out of fear that he might get into trouble again if left to his own devices.

This could very well be the reason why Greg had pleaded with her to join them. But, as far as she was concerned, seeing how distant Hallam was, how cool, how unwelcoming, the whole holiday was going to be a disaster. She really ought not to have come.

Almost as though he had read her thoughts, as though he could see inside her head and observe everything that was going on, Hallam said, 'What made you decide you'd like to holiday with us?'

Abby shrugged. 'Greg seemed so eager, and it's been a long time since I—'

'Greg!' he cut in sharply, incredulously. 'It's because of Greg?'

And not himself—that's what he was saying. He had wanted to believe that she had agreed to the holiday because of him! Abby had to smile and would have loved to confuse him further and say that yes it was because of his son. But she couldn't. She simply shook her head. 'It's because I need a holiday, that's all. And Greg's offer came at the right time. I gather you wouldn't have suggested it yourself?'

'What do you think?' he countered, dark eyes watching her face intently. He wore fawn cotton trousers and a white half sleeved shirt which emphasised the deep tan he had already miraculously acquired.

'I think you were glad that the case was over and it was the last you would see of me,' she answered, while thinking that he looked, if possible, more devastating than ever, and she wondered how she was going to get through the next two weeks without giving herself away.

'But you thought you'd scrape a few more pennies out of me,' he thrust derisively. 'What would a holiday like this be worth, I wonder? A beautiful, spacious villa overlooking the Med, every possible convenience, all meals found, maid service, car at your disposal.'

He paused and looked at her thoughtfully, one eyebrow crookedly raised. 'A lot of money, wouldn't you say? A hell of a lot of money in fact. Yes, I can see why you made your decision.'

Long before he had finished Abby was fuming. 'How dare you?' she cried. 'If you want me to pay for the holiday then I will. And if you feel so strongly then you should have told Greg that it wasn't a good idea. You didn't have to go along with it.'

'No, I didn't, did I?' he said, and his lip curled in a sudden smile. 'I simply thought it might be—interesting.'

'Interesting?' she echoed. 'What is that supposed to mean?' Surely not that he was going to spend his time amusing himself at her expense?

'I think you know,' he said darkly.

Abby shifted uncomfortably in her seat. At least it appeared that he wasn't totally against her joining them. But she could not afford to enter into any sort of affair that would end the instant the holiday was over. And how about the French woman? Where did she enter into things? It was all very unsettling.

'Can you fly this plane yourself?' she asked in a deliberate attempt to change the conversation.

'Oh, yes,' he answered. 'I got my pilot's licence many years ago.'

'Do you use it in the course of your job?'

'Sometimes,' he told her. 'It depends how far I'm going. I use it mainly for pleasure.'

'How long have you owned your villa?'

He smiled, seeming amused by her many questions. 'Twelve years. Is this the solicitor side of you, Sommers, or are you always this inquisitive?'

Abby looked at him in surprise. 'I'm sorry; I was just making conversation. You don't have to tell me anything you don't want to.'

'Perhaps we should talk about you.' He paused a moment and watched the widening of her incredible green eyes. 'Let's start with how old you were when you had your first boyfriend.'

She gasped. 'Goodness, that's unfair. I didn't ask you personal questions.'

'But maybe you would have liked to,' he commented, watching her reaction closely.

Abby could not hide the look of guilt in her eyes. Of course she had wanted to ask him—about his wife, about his French girlfriend, about all manner of things. 'I obviously have better manners than you,' she retorted defensively.

'Or less nerve,' he said with a surprising chuckle. 'Aren't you going to tell me?'

She shrugged. 'OK, if you wish.' And she gave an inward smile. 'I had my first boyfriend when I was five years old. We started school together and vowed we would get married when we grew up. His name was Adrian Beckett and he—'

'That wasn't exactly what I asked,' he cut in, pretending to be annoyed, but she could see by the light in his eyes that he saw the funny side of it. 'I'm talking about real boyfriends.'

Abby turned down the corners of her mouth thoughtfully. 'OK, let me see… There was Tony and Brian, then Andy, then Wayne, and after him there was Robert—oh, and John. I nearly forgot John; he was fun. And then there was Chris and—'

'You've had that many boyfriends?' Again he butted in but this time he definitely looked shocked.

Abby laughed at his expression. 'Of course I haven't; I haven't had time. It's been hard work getting where I am today. It's just that I object to being questioned about my private life.'

He looked at her long and hard now. 'So there's never been anyone serious? I find that hard to believe. I cannot imagine that—'

'You'd better believe it,' she cut in firmly, her eyes level on his, 'because it's true. Can't we talk about something else?' It was difficult to see why he was so interested in her.

'We shall soon be there.'

Abby looked out and could see, far below, the countryside of France, the green and gold of the fields and the occasional glint of water. She was glad to have her attention diverted away from Hallam. All too soon she would be meeting his lady-friend. Soon her holiday would begin. Soon she would know whether it was going to be enjoyable or unbearable.

The plane put down at a tiny private airfield and in no time at all they were speeding on their way in an open-topped red sports car.

Late summer had turned hot in England over recent days but it was even worse here; it was humid and sticky and Abby was glad of the cooling breeze as the car raced along. Impulsively she took the clips out of her hair and let it blow and she felt wonderfully free, as though she was leaving her past behind and starting a new life with this man.

A new life! With Hallam! What a stupid thought. Where on earth had that come from? Besides, there would be Greg and the French girl ever present; she would probably see nothing of this hunk of a man who was sitting at her side now and turning her thoughts upside down.

'I prefer your hair loose,' he said surprisingly. 'You look about eighteen.'

'I'm actually considering having it cut,' she told him. It was such a nuisance sometimes, and she was quite seriously thinking about a new image—probably because Hallam constantly said that she looked nothing like a solicitor.

'No!' His response was surprisingly strong. 'You mustn't; it's your most attractive feature. I have a painting by Titian and the girl looks remarkably like you. A little rounder, a little plumper, perhaps—but she has the same wonderful hair.'

Abby felt confused, she wasn't used to flattery from this man—at least, not on this scale—and she was glad when he turned off the main road and began threading his way along a series of leafy lanes. They came out on a headland, near the coast and a residential settlement that looked as though it was Millionaires' Row. She couldn't quite believe her eyes.

Each property overlooked the Mediterranean, none was near enough to its neighbour to be intrusive, and each looked large enough to house a whole army of people. And one of these was Hallam's holiday villa! Some villa, she thought as he drove along a private road, finally pulling up in front of the very last house.

It was not the largest but it was certainly impressive, with marble pillars along the whole of the front elevation—like soldiers on guard, she thought. He lifted her suitcase from the back seat and she followed him around to the other side of the property, which she soon realised was semicircular in shape. It overlooked the azure waters of the Mediterranean, and a series of steep steps led down to a crescent-shaped beach. The villa also boasted its own pool, and Greg, who was swimming, suddenly spotted them and came racing over to greet her.

He hauled himself out and looked suddenly shy. 'Hello, Miss Sommers; I'm glad you're here.' He was thin but wiry, and the sun glinted off the water streaming down his already lightly tanned body.

'Abby,' she reminded him. 'And I'm glad to be here as well.' I think, she added silently. Only time would tell. 'I never imagined anywhere like this. It's out of this world.'

Greg continued to look at her awkwardly and Abby wondered whether he was embarrassed because he was wearing only brief swimming trunks whereas she and his father were fully dressed.

'I'll take Miss Sommers up to her room,' said Hallam, his tone suddenly brusque. 'Tell Jaime I'm back and that we'd like tea on the terrace in ten minutes.'

Abby was whisked away before she could say anything else, through a house that was all cool elegance and marbled walls and floors, though she was given no time to admire or study it. For some reason known only to himself he seemed to be in a terrible hurry.

There were exotic leafy plants everywhere and yards of white muslin drapes at the windows, as well as very necessary shutters. Abby was thankful for the air-conditioning and knew that she would not be able to sit outside for long spells at a time; her fair skin would not take it.

Upstairs several doors led off a central semicircular landing, and each door had a gold and enamel flower motif set in the glowing wood. A white lily was on the one that Hallam opened and inside was a huge, airy room, again with marble floors, and walls in palest green; everything else was white—lily-white.

Abby wondered whether each room was decorated in the same colour as the flower on its door. It was an intriguing thought. Surprisingly, considering its pale decor, the room was beautiful—not at all austere or clinical as one might have imagined. It was so different from her own cosy little house with its wealth of colour that

Abby could only stand and stare. It was probably the space that impressed her most.

'You don't like it?'

She had almost forgotten Hallam standing at her side. 'Oh, yes—I'm sorry—I do; of course I do. It's—wonderful.' It was a totally inadequate word to describe the room's understated elegance, but for once in her life words failed her.

He set her suitcase down on a long, low stool with gilt legs which stood at the end of the bed. 'Bathroom through there,' he announced. 'Don't bother to unpack; Jamie will do that for you later. Though, I've no doubt you'll wish to change into something cooler. We'll be out on the terrace when you're ready.'

He disappeared and Abby was left to look and wonder. How the other half live, she thought. His home in England had impressed her with its security gates and high walls, but this was something else, and she could not believe that he used it only for holidays. Unless his girlfriend lived here—permanently? Jaime was obviously the maid and there was no sign of anyone else at the moment, but how long would it be before she met the girl with the sexy voice?

The floor-to-ceiling windows pushed open onto a balcony which ran along the whole length of the building. The only boundary between each bedroom was a row of potted plants. Abby wasn't sure that she was happy about that. It meant that anyone could step out of one bedroom and into another without the other occupants of the house knowing. She would definitely make sure that she kept her windows locked.

Or was she worrying for nothing, setting up obstacles that weren't there? Surely Hallam Lane wouldn't dare intrude on her privacy, not when he already had a girlfriend? She shook the thought free. It was a magical place; she was glad Greg had invited her here, and she was not going to let anything spoil it.

She took a quick shower in a bathroom that was bigger than her bedroom at home, again all in white and the softest of greens, with huge, fluffy towels and every conceivable toiletry product that she could wish for.

As it was the hottest part of the day Abby knew she needed to cover up and decided to wear a long-sleeved cream linen shift, cool and loose and comfortable. There was no point in courting trouble this early in her holiday. She teemed it with a narrow gilt belt and flat gold sandals, and after brushing her hair back into a band she made her way down to the men.

Greg gave a broad smile of welcome; Hallam eyed her thoroughly, especially her hair, and then invited her to take a drink of iced tea.

He too had changed out of his shirt and trousers and wore only a pair of well-cut white shorts. His powerfully muscled chest was as deeply tanned as his face, as were his legs, which were covered with fine dark hairs. Abby found it difficult to keep her eyes off him.

She had to force herself to look at the table. By this time she was absolutely starving and wondered what time they were having lunch. There wasn't even a biscuit to nibble with their drink and her stomach gave a loud grumble of protest.

Hallam unfortunately heard. 'Lunch is in half an hour,' he said. 'Didn't you have breakfast?'

Abby shook her head.

'Because you couldn't wait to get here?' he taunted.

Abby hoped he wasn't still under the impression that she wanted to have a good time at his expense. 'Too nervous, as a matter of fact,' she said unthinkingly.

Hallam frowned. 'Of what—flying?'

'No.'

'Then what is there to be nervous of?'

You, she wanted to say; you and my unstoppable thoughts. In the plane, and here now—in fact whenever he was anywhere near—she could not stop her adrenalin flowing, could not stop a deep gut feeling that said she wanted to go to bed with this man.

She still refused to believe that it was love. How could she love someone who treated her so casually, who more often than not seemed to despise her? Nevertheless, it was a strong attraction she felt and—rightly or wrongly—it was what had brought her out here!

'I don't wish to be an unwanted guest,' she told him finally.

Thick brows rose, as though he did not believe her, but before he could speak Greg cut in. 'You're not unwanted, Abby. Is she, Father? You've said before that this house needs filling with people.'

He had probably planned to fill it with his own offspring, thought Abby. He had probably never expected that he would spend most of his holidays here alone. It was a wonder he hadn't sold it—unless he used it as a love-nest. The thought was disquieting.

'That's right, Greg,' replied Hallam, but the suggestion was there that he would have preferred them to be people of his own choice. 'Lemon with your tea, Sommers?'

'Please.' It hurt when he spoke to her so curtly and she glanced cautiously at Greg while his father was busy with the jug. He smiled sympathetically, as though well aware of her pained thoughts, even though Abby was positive that he could have no real idea how deep her feelings ran.

She returned his smile and then looked at Hallam and he was watching them frowningly. 'Thank you,' she said, accepting the glass from him.

'I think it's time you got showered, Greg,' said Hallam, his voice suddenly sharp, 'if you don't want to be late for lunch.'

The young man looked unwilling to leave but dutifully did as his father suggested, and when he had gone Abby could not help saying, 'Why did you send him away? It won't take him a whole half-hour to get showered. I was looking forward to having a chat with him.'

'There will be plenty of time for talking,' he told her distantly. 'Is it younger men you prefer?'

Abby's eyes widened. 'What do you mean?'

'You said you came here because of Greg. I saw the way you were looking at each other just now. I'm not a fool, Sommers, so don't take me for one. I suppose this is the reason he was so insistent that you prepare his case. Is it mutual?'

Abby could not believe she was hearing this. 'You're crazy. Me and Greg? I'm eleven years older than he is, for heaven's sake.'

'I can't see that making any difference.'

She let out a little hiss of anger. 'If this is an indication of what the holiday is going to be like then I've made a serious mistake. It will be no pleasure if you accuse me of trying to seduce your son every time I speak to him.' It was so ludicrous. How could he possibly think such a thing?

'Let's hope I'm wrong,' he said loftily. 'More tea?'

Abby had not even touched the glass he'd poured her and she shook her head. 'No, thanks. Is anyone else staying here?'

He frowned; it was his turn to be surprised by her question. 'No. Why do you ask?'

She shrugged. 'I just wondered.' His answer pleased her. 'Do you have people drop in?'

'You're wondering whether we're going to be alone all the time, is that it?' he asked, comprehension dawning in his eyes.

'It's a big house.'

'You think, maybe, I entertain a host of girlfriends?'

He was so uncannily accurate that Abby found herself colouring. 'Not exactly a host.'

'But you do think that I—er—amuse myself while I'm here?' He paused, watching her closely. 'What gave you that impression?'

Abby's lips twisted wryly. Why did she always run herself into a corner? Why couldn't she keep her thoughts to herself? She lifted her shoulders. 'The girl who answered the telephone—I thought—'

'Jaime!' he exclaimed. 'You thought Jaime was my lover?'

Abby nodded. It looked as though she was well and truly making a fool of herself. Except that when she'd phoned the villa she had not known he'd got a maid, and when he did mention it she hadn't connected her with the voice on the end of the line.

'An interesting theory.' He seemed suddenly amused. 'What would you say if she was?'

'It would be none of my business,' she retorted sharply.

'That's right,' he said. 'It wouldn't.'

When Jaime, a petite, very pretty, dark-haired girl, came out a few minutes later to take away their empty glasses and announce that lunch was ready Abby could not help noticing how her expressive brown eyes lingered on her employer.

He politely introduced them and Jaime gave her a sharp smile, as though weighing her up, wondering what sort of a threat she posed. Maybe Hallam wasn't interested in her, but it looked as though the girl was most definitely interested in him.

It wasn't until much later that Abby realised Hallam had not actually denied that he was involved with the French girl.

CHAPTER SEVEN

ABBY was almost afraid to look at Greg during their meal, or even talk to him. It was totally ludicrous that Hallam Lane should think she was interested in his son. His *son* of all people!

She found it hard to believe that he had jumped to that conclusion. It made no sense, and if she was forced to watch what she was doing or saying to Greg for the whole of the next two weeks it would be no holiday at all. Not that it had promised to be a good one, but at least she had thought that she would have only her own feelings to contend with.

On top of that, each time Jaime came into the room her eyes narrowed thoughtfully on Abby. There had to be something going on here, she decided—something Hallam wasn't telling her. Why else would the girl look at her so suspiciously and hostilely?

Did she live in? Was she more than just a daily maid? Was she a permanent part of this household? The very thought that she could creep into Hallam's bedroom via the balcony in the middle of the night without anyone knowing made Abby's blood run cold.

After lunch Hallam suggested they all take a siesta, but Abby could not sleep. She could not even rest; her mind was in too much turmoil. In the end she got up off her bed, pulled on a straw hat that she had bought during her last holiday abroad, and, after tiptoeing downstairs, quietly let herself out of the house.

The blue pool looked inviting but the sea even more so, and she decided to explore beyond the boundaries of the property. Well-worn wooden steps zigzagged steeply down the cliff to the shore below. Dangerous if you'd had a few drinks, thought Abby, carefully holding onto the handrail until she finally reached the bottom.

The curved headland sheltered the bay and each villa appeared to have its own private section of beach. Everywhere was deserted. At one end was a small marina with several very expensive-looking yachts.

Abby wondered idly whether one of them belonged to Hallam and she spent several minutes looking at the names, trying to decide which might be his. She thought perhaps *Fast Lady,* or *Emma-Jane;* they were the only two with English-sounding names.

On the verge of heading back the way she had come and maybe dabbling her feet in the tempting waters of the ocean, Abby suddenly heard a male voice coming from one of the boats. 'A vision of beauty, no less, come to torment me.'

Having thought they were all empty, Abby looked in startled surprise to see who was speaking. He spoke in English, whoever he was, and a head suddenly appeared from *Fast Lady,* followed by a long, lean body, deeply tanned and clad in no more than a pair of frayed, cut-off faded denims that looked as though they should have been thrown in the rag-bin many months ago.

It was not quite the attire she would have expected of someone living in one of these exclusive villas. Maybe he didn't. Maybe he was a mechanic come to repair the engine. But he had a friendly face all the same and she gave him a wide smile. 'Hello there; I didn't realise any-one was about.'

'English as well,' he said. 'This really is my day.' He vaulted off the yacht and came towards her, holding out his hand, white teeth gleaming. 'Rod Duvall.' He had short, spiky blond hair and blue eyes and was about her own age.

'Abby Sommers,' she said, and his handshake was firm and unnecessarily long.

'Abby?' He seemed to savour the word. 'A delightful name for a delightful lady. I love auburn hair. God, you're beautiful.'

'And you're nothing but a smooth-talking flatterer,' she said with a laugh, but the compliment pleased her nevertheless.

'Where have you come from? What are you doing here? How long are you staying? No ring, I see; I cannot believe my good fortune.'

The questions came thick and fast and Abby shook her head, still laughing. 'Are you always like this? Are you always so curious?'

'Only when it's someone as beautiful as you,' he said solemnly. 'And then why hesitate? Say what you think. Life's too short for dilly-dallying. Is there a man on the scene? Am I out of luck—yet again?' he added with a resigned air.

'Actually there is no one,' Abby told him, seeing no reason why she shouldn't be totally honest. 'I'm here with Hallam Lane and his son—a sort of thank-you for something I did for them.'

Rod's grin almost split his face in two. He looked like the original Cheshire cat. 'I like the sound of this more and more. What are you doing tonight?'

Abby wanted to laugh at his impetuosity, but instead

she tilted her chin and gave him a hard, questioning look. 'Maybe I should ask you a few questions, Mr Rod Duvall. For all I know you could be happily married with two children.'

'I'm not, I promise,' he said, continuing to grin. 'I'm as free as the air. My parents own that villa there—the second from the end—and I was supposedly coming out with a girlfriend, but she ditched me at the last minute. So I came anyway.'

'Are you alone in the house, or are your parents here as well?' She liked this man—he was a refreshing change. But he also gave the impression of being quite a womaniser, and she had no intention of getting mixed up with him.

'Gosh, yes, my parents are at home. They wouldn't trust me here alone; they think I would have wild orgies and wreck the place.' He spread his hands expansively. 'As if I would.'

'You do look a bit wild to me,' said Abby, laughing as she spoke.

'Because I don't always conform? Hell, life's for living; why not make the most of it? I guess one day I'll settle down and have the statistical two point four children, but meanwhile I intend to have fun.'

'Do you work?' she asked. If his parents were rich enough to afford a villa here, maybe they spoiled him too. He looked the sort to spend his time backpacking around the world, doing nothing in particular at all.

'I'm not a rich playboy if that's what you think,' he answered easily. 'I have to earn my own bread; my parents don't give me a penny. I'm an insurance broker, for my sins.'

Abby laughed yet again. 'You don't look anything like one.'

'A typical response,' he groaned. 'Would you like me to put on a grey suit and tie and slick back my hair? Would that convince you?'

She shook her head. 'You needn't go that far; I believe you.'

'Good. May I ask what you do for a living?'

Abby contained a smile, knowing that she would get exactly the same reaction. 'I'm a solicitor,' she answered demurely.

His blue eyes widened. 'No! Really? You're kidding. You're having me on.'

'No, it's true,' she answered with conviction.

'There you are, then,' he said. 'We're made for each other. Two serious working people ready to let our hair down the moment we're set free. How about tonight? We could—'

'I don't think so,' cut in Abby swiftly. 'It's my first day here.' Hallam would probably have a fit if she said she was going out with a complete stranger. And although Rod looked like fun she didn't actually fancy him, and wasn't altogether sure that she could trust him.

Rod shrugged easily. 'Another time, then. Maybe the three of you could come round for drinks one evening; then we can get to know each other. My parents would be delighted, I know. I believe they know Hallam Lane quite well. Can't say I've had the pleasure myself. What's he like?'

'Tall, broad-shouldered, good-looking, dark-haired,' she provided.

'His wife's not with him?'

'He's a widower.'

'Ah!' he commented thoughtfully, and it was easy to see what was going through his mind. 'How old is he?'

Abby laughed. 'Around forty, I guess, but he's not interested in me, if that's what you're thinking.'

'Good!' he said with conviction. 'I should hate to have to fight off the opposition.'

Abby decided she had said enough and when suddenly Hallam's loud voice hailed her from the cliff top she said a quick goodbye and ran back towards the steps.

She reached the top, out of breath and perspiring freely, conscious that Hallam had watched her every inch of the way. His black brows were knitted ferociously together, eyes as hard as polished jet. 'Who was that you were talking to?'

'He said he was a neighbour,' she answered, surprised by how angry he looked. Surely talking to one of the Duvalls wasn't a crime?

Hallam frowned. 'He's not one I've ever seen. You really should be careful. And, in any case, you should not have left the house without telling me.'

Abby's eyes flashed. 'Did you really expect me to come to your bedroom and say I was going out?'

'You could have left a message with Jaime.'

'No one was about,' she retorted.

'Only fools go out in this heat.'

'Then I'm a fool,' she said. 'But I couldn't rest; I decided to have a look around. Surely there's no harm in that?'

His eyes were still hard on hers. 'I was watching you. The two of you seemed to be getting on pretty well together. What were you talking about? Did he ask if he could take you out?'

Abby's chin lifted and her green eyes flashed. 'As a matter of fact, yes, he did. Do you have a problem with that?'

Hallam let out his breath in a savage hiss. 'Yes, I do have a problem. What did you say?'

'I refused him.'

He looked slightly appeased, but not much.

'For the moment,' she added defiantly.

He took her by the shoulders then and shook her as though she were a child he had caught doing wrong. 'Hell, Sommers, you don't know him.'

'I hardly know you either; what's the difference?' she asked coolly, lifting her chin and staring at him, at the same time experiencing a thrill of pleasure at his touch. 'I've taken just as much of a risk coming here as I would on a date with Rod Duvall.'

'Duvall?' His fingers dug into her shoulder blades just that little bit more firmly

'You know him, then?' she asked.

'I know his—family.'

'Rod suggested the three of us might like to go over for drinks one evening.'

'I don't think so,' said Hallam curtly.

'You don't like them?'

'It's not that; it's just that—well, I have my own reasons.'

Which he wasn't going to tell her! There were lots of things he wasn't telling her.

'And I want you to promise me that you won't go out with him.'

Abby tried unsuccessfully to twist free. 'I don't see why I should. You're not my keeper.'

'Nevertheless I feel responsible for you while you're here.'

Her brows rose sceptically. Hallam, responsible for her? That had to be a joke. 'I'm sure he has no deep dark intentions,' she insisted. 'He seems like fun, as a matter of fact.'

'One can never be too sure,' he warned.

Abby looked down at the beach and Rod was still standing where she had left him, watching them, and probably wondering whether she had told him the truth about her relationship with Hallam. She increased her struggles to escape. 'I don't have to answer to you,' she said strongly. 'If I want to go out with Rod then I will.'

Lord knew why she was saying these things when she had no intention of dating the blond-haired man. But Hallam angered her and she wanted to hit back—and she wished he would let her go. She deeply resented his telling her what she should or should not do.

With alarming suddenness his mouth came down on hers. Abby was totally unprepared and it burst upon her like a flash-fire, enveloping and consuming, blowing her mind, filling her with desire—all within the space of a few seconds!

'Hallam!' she managed to choke out against his lips. 'What are you doing?'

'What I've wanted to do ever since I picked you up this morning,' he muttered thickly.

Abby gave a start of surprise, but his mouth had already claimed hers again, making further talk impossible. He had certainly given no impression that he wanted to kiss her—in fact quite the opposite. She felt sure that his actions now were only because Rod Duvall was watching them. Perhaps it was his way of warning the other man off, pretending that she was his property. He could not know that she had already told their neighbour otherwise.

Whatever, her whole body was being consumed by a total hunger that paid no heed to common sense, and of their own volition her arms snaked around him and her lips parted to his probing tongue.

This was the real reason she had come out here, not the fact that she needed a holiday. Not that Greg needed her. But because she needed Hallam! Her body heated to furnace-like proportions, every bone ached, her head fell back on her shoulders; she was pliant in his arms, returning his kisses with an ardour that must have surprised Hallam and which frightened herself.

She urged her body against his, felt the power of his arousal and then, like a replay of the last time they had kissed, he abruptly put her from him. 'Greg is waiting for you to join him in the pool,' he said, a cold edge to his voice now.

It was as though he had thrown a bucket of icy water over her. Desire vanished and her eyes widened in confusion. 'So what was that all about?' she asked in a frozen whisper.

'It was an unfortunate mistake,' he growled. 'Forget it ever happened.'

'A mistake?' she queried. 'A mistake? Are you quite sure about that? Or was it a show put on for the benefit of Rod Duvall?'

He frowned harshly, as if wondering what she was talking about, and then he looked down at the beach and Rod was just striding away. 'Duvall had nothing to do with it,' he announced brusquely.

But Abby was not so sure. There had been no other reason for him to kiss her right here in full view of the younger man. Hallam did not strike her as the sort to show his feelings in public; he would have chosen a much more private place had he wanted to kiss her.

And if he had been of that mind earlier why hadn't he kissed her then? What had stopped her? No, it definitely had something to do with Rod Duvall. And it was hardly likely now that Rod would ask her out again. Hallam had most definitely made a statement.

She threw him a caustic, impatient glance and, turning her back on him, headed for the pool, not even waiting to see whether he followed.

Greg looked up at her with an easy grin as she approached. 'Where have you been? I was looking for you. It's wonderful in here. Get yourself changed and come and try it.'

What a different reaction from his father's! Why couldn't they both have been the same? What a wonderful holiday it would have been then. Abby threw him a warm smile. 'Won't be a minute.' And she ran into the house.

As she wriggled out of her shift and pulled on a black and green geometrically patterned swimsuit Abby could not help pondering over Hallam's unreasonable reaction to Rod. It couldn't altogether be because he objected to her speaking to this other man, she felt sure. Maybe he did not like the Duvalls and therefore his antagonism extended to their son as well.

If this was the case it was a very intolerant view. How could he know what the young man was like if he had never met him? She was half inclined to go out with Rod—if he ever asked her again—purely out of bloody-mindedness. At least she would have fun—it looked as though everything was going to be heavy going where Hallam Lane was concerned.

Uppermost in her mind, however, was her body's reaction to his kiss. It had created a whirlpool effect inside her, stirring her senses to such a degree that she had been unable to stop herself responding. She really would have to learn to control her feelings; otherwise he would assume he could kiss her wherever and whenever he felt like it. And although it would be beautiful while it lasted she did not relish the thought of the heartache she would suffer afterwards.

The water was cooling and refreshing, a balm to her troubled thoughts, and she swam a few lazy lengths, and one full length under water, before realising that Hallam had joined them. She came up for air and he was next to her. 'You're a good swimmer, Sommers,' he said, his dark eyes unfathomable, so that she had no idea whether he was still angry with her or not.

'It's good of you to say so,' she responded, before setting off again for the other end of the pool, again under water.

When she reached it he was there before her. 'You swim like a fish, or maybe I should say a mermaid.' And now she saw that the ill-humour had definitely gone; there was admiration on his face, an approving curve to his lips.

Abby's hair hung down her back like a silken curtain, much darker than usual, but still with a distinctive auburn sheen. She had no idea how beautiful she looked and found it difficult to accept that he was paying her these compliments.

'Maybe I should find you a rock to sit on?' he suggested, his brows quirking.

'And maybe you should leave me alone,' Abby snapped, the words out before she could stop them. He had been so scathing a few minutes ago; how was she supposed to react, for goodness' sake? He was such an impossible man; how was she supposed to accept the difference in him now?

Greg, who had just that moment joined them from the other end of the pool, looked at her both questioningly and worriedly. Unaware of the harsh words they had exchanged earlier, he could not understand her reaction to his father.

She gave the boy a reassuring smile. 'Come on, Greg. I'll race you.'

She was off in a flash, but not before she had seen Hallam's frown of disapproval. When they reached the other end, Greg only a second behind her, she looked back and Hallam had gone.

'What's the problem between you and my father?' Greg asked as they hauled themselves up onto the edge and sat with their feet dangling in the water. 'I was hoping that now the case was over you'd be friends.'

'I don't think we'll ever be that,' she told him sorrowfully.

He sighed. 'Do you hate him?'

Abby grimaced and gave a faint smile. 'I wouldn't say I hate him exactly, but we're hardly compatible. I find him a difficult man to understand.' The sun was hot on her back and common sense told her that she mustn't sit here for too long.

Greg nodded. 'He's different from what he used to be. Before he and my mother separated he was great fun, the best father anyone could ever have. He was always playing with me and taking me out and helping me with my schoolwork. I thought we'd be mates for ever.'

He heaved a sigh and was quiet for a moment before carrying on. 'Don't get me wrong; we still love each other. But he changed when Mum left and he couldn't get permanent custody of me; he grew bitter and much more serious, and after she died and I came back to live with him he seemed somehow disappointed in me. We have our moments, naturally, and on the whole we get on well. But there are times...' He let his voice fade away. 'This last lot of trouble hasn't helped.'

'I think what truly worries your father is that you have no ambition,' Abby said quietly and tentatively. 'Have you no plans for when you leave university?'

'Not really,' he confessed, thrashing the water with his feet.

'Isn't there anything that interests you?' She watched the changing patterns of light and shade across the heaving surface. 'How about following in his footsteps?'

Greg shook his head. 'I'm not interested in buying and selling, although—' and he said it wistfully '—I would like to study gems from a scientific point of view.'

She looked at him with interest. 'And you've told your father this?'

Again he shook his head. 'He'd put me down. It's hardly a get-rich-quick type of profession.'

'And that's all Hallam is interested in—making money?' she queried with a sudden frown.

Greg shrugged. 'You've seen our house, and this place, and he has an apartment in London. Money is everything to my father.'

Abby frowned. She had never thought this about Hallam and yet she supposed he did live a fairly luxurious lifestyle. Nevertheless she was not sure that she agreed with Greg. 'Do you think your parents would have got back together if your mother hadn't died?' she asked him softly, hesitantly.

He shrugged, looking troubled all of a sudden. 'Who's to say? He never forgave her for going off with someone else.'

'Do you think he'll ever remarry?'

Again he lifted his shoulders. 'I doubt it. I actually wish he would. I don't like to see him so lonely.'

'I guess she would have to be someone very special,' Abby ventured.

'Very special,' admitted Greg gruffly.

After that they changed the subject, Abby asking Greg about his friends. He told her a joke that made her laugh heartily and soon they were exchanging jokes, and Abby thought that this was how a holiday should be—light-hearted and fun, with no cross words or undercurrents.

Suddenly the hairs on the back of her neck prickled and she got the feeling that she was being watched—and watched far too intently for her peace of mind! Very casually Abby let her eyes wander, and there was Hallam—up on the balcony, standing with his hands resting on the stone coping, dark eyes narrowed and disapproving as he watched the two of them enjoying themselves.

'I think it's time to swim again,' she said, 'before I get burnt to a frazzle.' She leaned forward and dived into the cool, clear water, and the next time she glanced upwards the balcony was empty.

Abby swam several punishing lengths before declaring she'd had enough. Greg called her a chicken and continued to swim but she climbed out and flopped onto one of the several loungers that were conveniently arranged beneath the shade of blue and white umbrellas. It felt good to relax.

A few minutes later Abby sensed someone standing beside her and, expecting it to be Greg, she looked up with a ready smile, startled to discover that it was his father instead—Greg himself was nowhere in sight. Her sixth sense had not warned her this time! Her smile faded and her heartbeats increased.

A bottle of sun-lotion was balanced on Hallam's palm and he tossed it to her.

'Thank you,' she said, somewhat surprised by his thoughtfulness.

'Don't underestimate the power of the sun even in the shade,' he warned. He had changed from his swimming trunks back into his shorts and to her dismay he lay down next to her. Her peace was well and truly disturbed. There would be no relaxing now.

As Abby sat up to smooth the lotion into her already overheated skin she saw that his eyes were closed, and without even realising it she paused and studied him, feeling a tingling in her nerve-endings as she let her eyes rake over that magnificent male body. There was not an ounce of superfluous fat on him; he was lean and lithe, muscles taut, dark hairs curling softly on his chest, arrowing down towards...

Her heart beat even faster as she recalled the pulsing power of his manhood pressed against her only a short time earlier, and she moved her gaze quickly to his legs, sliding down their powerful length, and then back up to his face.

'Do you like what you see?'

Swift colour flooded Abby's cheeks. His eyes weren't closed after all! Lord, what could she say? What was he thinking? How could she explain herself?

She lifted her shoulders and made a great show out of squeezing some more of the thick, creamy lotion into her palm. 'You're no different from other men,' she said, trying to sound matter of fact.

'And do you study them all in so personal a manner?' he questioned. 'If you do you could be asking for trouble, my girl.'

'You're imagining things,' she said brittlely. 'I was merely admiring your suntan.'

His lips quirked. 'Not good enough, Sommers. I know exactly what you were doing. Would you like any help?'

'No, thanks,' she retorted, still feeling deeply embarrassed.

'I could do your back,' he said, his tone softly persuasive all of a sudden.

She shook her head. 'I can manage.'

'As you wish.' And he settled down again, but a smile continued to play about his lips.

Abby struggled now to spread the lotion between her shoulderblades. She had slipped off the straps to her swimsuit and bent her head forward to keep her hair out of the way. She did not see Hallam rise, or suspect that he had moved towards her, knew nothing in fact until his hand touched her back. A searing heat ran through her. 'What are you doing?' she asked in alarm.

'Helping,' he murmured, his voice like a caress over her skin.

Some help, she thought. It was panic stations inside her. 'I told you I can manage,' she protested.

'It doesn't look that way to me,' he pointed out, 'and since I've started I might as well carry on. Why don't you lie down and make yourself comfortable?'

Abby decided it would be easier to comply than argue and she reluctantly manoeuvred herself onto her stomach, resting her forehead on her arms and tensing herself for his assault.

'Relax,' he muttered as first of all he stroked her hair out of the way, seeming to find a great deal of pleasure in allowing the thick locks to slide silkily through his fingers. It was almost dry.

'I am relaxed,' she retorted.

'You could have fooled me.' He picked up the bottle and dribbled some lotion onto her back, and then began a slow, purposeful massage which was the worst form of torture imaginable.

Abby kept her eyes tightly closed and tried to keep her mind blank, but in vain. Every sense in her body was attuned to him, every nerve quivering, every pulse racing. He must surely be aware of it?

And then all of a sudden the pressure in his fingers increased, and a caustic note entered his voice. 'Did you enjoy your swim with my son?'

So that was what this was all about, she thought. Not a desire to touch her but to reprimand her. 'What do you mean, did I like it?' she asked. 'Of course I did; I love swimming.'

'Especially with Greg,' he taunted. 'And talking to him, and laughing and sharing, and being a completely different person.' His thumbs ran up her spine, his hands splayed firmly about her ribcage. Firm hands, hard hands. Abby had the feeling that she was about to be crushed. 'I don't want you encouraging him,' he growled. 'He is young and impressionable and—'

'What am I supposed to do—ignore him?' she asked, letting her breath out on a hiss of sheer disbelief. 'We're all three of us on holiday together; I see no harm in it. Will you please get your hands off me? I wish to go to my room.'

'Is that an excuse?'

'To what?' she asked.

'To escape me. Don't think I'm not aware of how your body reacts to mine. Maybe I have it wrong; maybe *I* am the reason you came out here—not Greg, not a so-called much-needed holiday, but a desire to have your basic needs fulfilled.'

She was lifted and turned onto her back with a suddenness that left her gasping. He bent over her, his eyes glittering, his hands on her shoulders, his breath warm on her cheek.

'How dare you?' she exclaimed. 'You couldn't be further from the truth. You're the last man I'd want anything to do with.'

'And I'm supposed to believe that, am I?' His eyes narrowed thoughtfully on hers. 'I'm sorry to disappoint you, my beautiful friend. Your body has told me many times what you want, even if your tongue lies. It is going to be my pleasure to oblige. This is definitely going to be a holiday to remember.' And with that his mouth closed on hers.

CHAPTER EIGHT

ABBY found it impossible to ignore the flurry of emotions set loose in her by Hallam's kiss, or the racing of her pulses, or the heat of her suddenly sensitised skin. She closed her eyes, as if by so doing she could shut out this tough-talking man who had the dangerous knack of reducing her to jelly.

It took tremendous will-power to keep her lips still under his, to lie like a marble statue, pretending indifference, knowing that this was the only way she could prove to him that he was wrong.

Eventually Hallam's frustration that he was getting no response communicated itself to her, and Abby began to feel a certain smugness, a sense of satisfaction that she was winning—until a renewed attack on her defences took her by surprise.

She hadn't been careful enough; he had felt the slight change in her, sensed her confidence that she was the victor, and his tongue suddenly parted her lips with an urgency that was frightening. At the same time he eased down her swimsuit, exposing her proudly erect breasts to his all-consuming eyes.

It was done before Abby could stop him, almost before she realised what he was doing, and she gave a shiver of sheer, unadulterated pleasure when one breast was cupped by a warm, firm, possessive male hand, possessed as intimately and confidently as if they were already lovers.

She gasped as her nipple surged and hardened beneath his touch, and although basic survival told her to resist basic desire forbade her. Instead of objecting she gave a whimper of pleasure, and by then it was too late. There was no going back, no denying that he had managed to arouse her.

'I think we need some privacy,' he muttered thickly, and with one swift, easy action he swung her up into his arms and strode towards the house. Abby did not utter a word. She was conscious only of her naked breasts brushing against his hair-roughened skin, of the closeness of his exciting, hard body, of the loud pumping of her heart—and his own echoing in response.

Not even when he climbed the stairs did she demur, nor when he carried her into his bedroom. She did not struggle or protest in any way—she was utterly incapable. It was as though he had taken over her mind.

When the door clicked shut behind them his mouth once more came down on hers. Abby linked her hands behind Hallam's neck and returned his kiss with a passion that—in that moment—did not even surprise her. It felt right—it was the reason she had come out here, the reason she had been so restless all day.

Nothing seemed to matter at this moment except gratification of a carnal need which was both new and alien to her. It was as though all sanity had fled. In fact she was not even thinking; she was letting herself be carried along by instinct alone.

She did not even stop to dwell on the fact that Hallam was playing a dangerous game, that he was trying to prove that her body was hungry for him. Such thoughts were lost in the proliferation of wild emotions that surged through her as his mouth continued to assault hers, as one hand still held captive an aching breast, a sure thumb stroking across her nipple, inducing further mind-blowing, heart-stopping sensations.

When he turned his attention to her other breast she still raised no objection, still she remained captive to her emotions. It was only when his lips left her mouth to burn an assault down the slender column of her throat, pausing a moment to press his tongue to the tell-tale flickering pulse at its base before tracing the high pointed curves of her breasts, that she made a faint murmur of protest.

But that was all it was—a murmur, a token gesture. As his tongue rasped this most sensitive part of her, teeth gently biting, mouth sucking, Abby gave herself up to the erotic pleasure of the moment, not wanting it to end. It was a unique experience, something she had never felt to this degree before.

Only fleetingly did the thought penetrate her mind that Hallam's reasons for making love to her had nothing to do with pleasure. Or so he had led her believe! It seemed to her that he was enjoying himself as much as she was. He too seemed gripped in a passion over which he had no control.

Quite how they made it to the bed Abby was not sure, but somehow she found herself lying there, the long, hard length of Hallam's body right next to her, one leg crooked over hers, one hand imprisoning her chin while his lips explored every curve of her face.

Tiny cries of satisfaction kept escaping her throat and when his tongue explored her mouth with an exciting urgency she involuntarily arched her body into his and her heart swelled as the evidence of his manhood made itself profoundly felt.

His mouth moved to make yet another attack on her breasts, his hand moulding their burgeoning fullness, his teeth nipping, tongue arousing. Abby held his head close, fingers threaded through his thick dark hair, her throat arched, her whole body aroused almost to fever-pitch, wallowing in the sensations that racked her body and were making her his.

Her hands raked over his back, nails digging into the silken hardness of his body, her hips unconsciously mov-ing, and it was not until his tongue worked its way along the flatness of her stomach, until his fingers began easing her swimsuit off altogether that the full significance of his actions made themselves clear.

She came back to the real world with a jolt, mentally shaking her head. What was she doing? What had hap-pened to her? Why had she let things go this far? *'Stop!'* Her green eyes blazed as she pushed at him now with savagely shaking hands. 'Get away from me!' Her heart, which had drummed with passionate desire a few sec-onds ago, now throbbed with violent anger.

For a fraction of a second he looked hurt, totally stunned by her sudden change of heart, as though it was the last thing he had expected—or wanted. But almost immediately a cynical smile took its place—so quickly in fact that Abby felt she must have imagined his initial reaction.

'I wondered how far you would let me go,' he drawled, eyes mocking now as he pushed himself up on one elbow.

'You swine!' Abby struggled to sit, her hand raised ready to strike him, but he was quicker and stronger and he caught her wrist in a vice-like grip, yanking her body against his, twisting her arm behind her back, effectively holding her prisoner. With his other hand he lifted her chin, his eyes challenging.

'Don't deny what you really want,' he growled. 'You're mine, all mine, whenever I care to take you. That's the real reason you came out here, isn't it?' He gave her no chance to answer. 'If it's lovemaking you're after, my passionate Sommers, then that's what you'll get.' He sounded angry now, and his mouth came down hard on hers once again.

Lord help her, thought Abby as she struggled ineffectively to free her mouth. Why, oh, why had she not fought like a wildcat in the very beginning? Why had she allowed his kisses? Why had she let him touch her so intimately?

She had permitted herself to be carried along on a tide of passion that equalled nothing she had experienced in the past, and now it looked as though she had to face the consequences! It was doubtful if Hallam would listen to protests or excuses; though, for the sake of her own sanity, she had to try and make him.

'It's not like that at all,' she insisted, managing finally to lift her chin and look up at him. But the action only served to thrust her breasts even harder against him, and the faint movement, the brushing of her nipples against his powerful chest, caused a further escalation of her pulses, a further upsurge of desire, followed quickly by panic!

Was this what sexual chemistry was all about—this wild abandonment of the body and mind? Was Hallam right? Was this the reason she had too eagerly accepted the invitation? Was this what she wanted from him?

No! No! her mind screamed. Never! She wanted love from him or nothing. She could not take this; she could not allow Hallam to use her body whenever he thought fit. She shook her head violently, copper hair swinging, eyes glowing. 'The last thing I'd do is holiday with a man for the sake of his body.'

Black brows rose, his dark eyes amused. 'I've not had very much evidence of it so far.'

Abby swallowed hard. It was incredible that she had almost allowed Hallam to make love to her on her first day. No wonder he was sceptical of her protests. How was she to get through another two weeks if he continued to press home his advantage? They would end up as lovers as sure as night followed day.

'Nothing more to say?' His thumb stroked her lower lip before pulling it down and dropping a kiss confidently inside.

Abby could not believe the sensations that ran unbounded through her; nothing seemed to stop them. She hated herself for being so weak, yet at the same time her body cried out for him.

It became suddenly imperative that she put distance between them, before he wore down her defences and started all over again. Fear injected her with strength and she wrenched herself free, raced for the door, yanked it open and charged along the corridor as though all the demons in hell were after her.

Greg was just coming up the stairs.

She caught a glimpse of his shocked face before bursting into her own room, slamming the door behind her and then leaning back against it as if to keep him out. Her chest was heaving, her fingers splayed over the cool paintwork, her head lolling back.

It was not until her breathing returned to normal, until she came back down to earth and opened her eyes that Abby realised her swimsuit was still down around her waist. Greg had seen all!

Humiliation washed over her. How could she face him after this? What interpretation would he put on it? More importantly, what would he think of his father? And herself? Dear Lord, why was this happening to her? Why was this holiday turning into a nightmare?

Suddenly she became aware of being watched. The same prickling sensation she had felt by the pool. Her eyes snapped towards the balcony—and Hallam! The doors were wide although she could not remember leaving them like that, and he stood looking at her without saying a word. And to her surprise he actually looked as though he deeply regretted the situation.

He couldn't, though, could he? He'd known exactly what he was doing; it had probably all been planned. 'If you've come to apologise, forget it,' she cried, rushing across the room in a blaze of fresh anger. She slammed the windows shut so fiercely that it was a wonder the glass did not shatter. And then she closed the shutters also so that he was well and truly locked out.

Curling her fingers into fists, she expelled her breath fiercely and loudly. 'Damn him!' she said to the room in general. 'Damn the man!'

Abby was so angry that she could hardly contain herself. How dared he do this to her? How dared he try to make out that she was to blame? He was the one who had started it; he was the one who had kissed her in the first place. Why couldn't he have left her alone, kept their relationship on a strictly impersonal level?

Tearing off her swimsuit, Abby headed for the shower, and stood for almost a quarter of an hour beneath its cooling jets, scrubbing herself furiously, but still feeling no better when she climbed out. She wanted to go home, desperately. Only pride stopped her. She

would not give him the satisfaction of calling her a cow-
ard.

She wiped the palm of her hand over the condensation
on the mirror and looked at herself, startled by the
brightness of her eyes, the high colour flaming her
cheeks. Her chin came up. She would see this thing
through if it killed her.

She would enjoy her holiday—she *would*. Mr Hallam
Lane could take a running jump; she wouldn't let him
touch her again. Not ever. She was prepared for him
now; she knew what he was like; she knew what she
had to do.

Their evening meal was an uncomfortable affair. Greg
looked at neither of them, keeping his eyes firmly fixed
on his plate. Hallam was wrapped in his own thoughts
and said not a word to him, even though he had no idea
that his son had seen Abby running from his room.

Abby conducted herself with quiet dignity, giving
nothing away of her churning emotions, of the heat that
still ran through her veins, and made a pretence of eating
even though she was not remotely hungry. Once or twice
she saw Hallam looking at her and gained the impression
that he wanted to say something, but because of his son
he was forced to remain silent.

When Greg finished he got up and walked out, still
without speaking, and Abby said quickly, 'He saw me,
you know, coming out of your room.'

Hallam groaned his dismay. 'That was most unfortunate. What did you say to him?'

'Nothing.'

'He saw your state of undress?'

Abby nodded.

Hallam ran a hand over his forehead. 'I must talk to
him.'

'Of course,' she muttered, unable to keep the sarcasm out of her voice. 'He must never believe that his father tried to force himself on me.'

Hallam's breath whistled through his teeth. 'You know as well as I do that's not true.'

'Isn't it?' she asked quietly, her eyes vividly green and full of derision. And before he could answer she screwed up her napkin, threw it down on the table and left the room also. She needed air and space, and plenty of it.

Outside it was not much cooler than it had been all day but there was no going back, however delicious the air-conditioning. She went quickly down the steps to the beach—and there, to her surprise, she met Greg. She had somehow expected him to shut himself away in his room.

He looked at her uneasily. 'I'm sorry.'

'Don't apologise,' she said kindly, hoping her own awkwardness did not show. 'It wasn't your fault you chose that moment to come up the stairs.'

'But I felt so embarrassed,' he mumbled, red-faced, shuffling his feet in the sand.

'So did I,' she said with a wry smile.

'I don't understand.' He looked at her again briefly. 'I thought you and my father didn't like each other very much?'

'Let's say it was a mistake,' she said positively. 'One which I shall make sure never happens again. Let's forget the whole thing.'

He heaved a sigh. 'I'd like to, but—if things are going to be like this between you and my father it won't be much of a holiday.' They walked together, Greg kicking the sand, still looking extremely unhappy about the whole situation.

Abby had never thought that her actions might affect Greg, although she had to agree with him—the holiday did look doomed to disaster. 'I am so sorry,' she said.

'Maybe I shouldn't have suggested you join us?' he responded.

'Neither of us knew it would lead to this,' she answered quietly.

But finally their conversation moved to less personal topics, and as they continued to walk and talk they gradually felt easier with each other and soon Abby was laughing over yet another one of Greg's endless jokes and she was telling him one of her great store of solicitor jokes. By the time they got back to the house they were both in much better spirits.

There was no sign of Hallam, but even so Abby took herself off to her room. She did not want to bump into him again today. She folded back the shutters and cautiously pushed open the doors to the balcony and peered out. He was still nowhere in sight, and with a sigh of relief she ventured out and sat down on one of the white-painted chairs, opening a magazine she had brought out with her from England.

Not surprisingly she could not concentrate, her thoughts returning over and over again to Hallam and the scene they had played out earlier. The more she thought about it the more ashamed she was of her actions. Why, oh, why had she allowed it? Why had she not fought him off in the very beginning? They were questions she knew she would never be able to answer. All she could do was make sure it didn't happen again.

It was a still, beautiful evening and the setting sun had turned the sky into a painting and the sea to molten gold. Abby was unaccustomed to such drama so close to hand and she got up and stood at the balustrade, watching as the sun gradually turned from palest gold to a deep blood-red, as the sea became a multitude of colours in the space of a few minutes—yellow, orange, and finally brilliant crimson shot through with purple.

A slight sound below caught her attention and when she looked down Abby was startled to discover that Hallam was sitting immediately beneath her, a glass in his hand, his attention also taken by nature's beauty unfolding itself before them.

Had he been there long? she wondered. Had he been sitting there when she and Greg had returned? This part of the courtyard was made private by a row of dense shrubs; they would not have been able to see him—but he would have most definitely heard them!

His voice suddenly rose up to her. 'Come down here, Sommers; I want to speak with you.'

She shrank back and pretended not to have heard but his voice came even louder.

'I know you are there,' he said. 'Come down here this minute.'

Abby considered disregarding him totally but knew that his voice would get progressively louder, until in the end she would be unable to ignore him. She leaned over the stonework and looked down.

'I'm sorry, I have no wish to talk to you,' she said in a sweet, soft voice that belied the strong feelings surging so violently inside her. 'I'm going to bed. Goodnight, Mr Lane.'

It had no effect. 'Goodnight be damned,' he returned, jumping to his feet and looking up at her. 'If you won't come down then I'll come up to you. There are things that need to be said.'

She gave a loud sigh that he could not fail to hear. 'Very well, but I can't see what's so important that it

can't wait till morning.' And her impatience still showed
on her face when she presented herself before him.

'A glass of wine?' he asked pleasantly.

Abby noticed there were two glasses beside the carafe
on the table. Only one had been used. Had it been his
intention all along to ask her to join him? Or had he
been expecting Jaime? Abby was still not one hundred
per cent sure that there was nothing going on between
him and the beautiful maid.

She shook her head. 'No, thanks.'

'Ever the abstainer,' he remarked sardonically.
'Please, sit down.'

Reluctantly she perched herself on the edge of one of
the wrought-iron chairs with their blue padded cushions.
'What have you got to say that's so urgent?'

He took a slow sip of the straw-coloured liquid, studying her intently over the rim of his glass as he did so,
an odd light gleaming in the dark depths of his eyes.
'What have you and Greg been up to?'

Abby frowned. 'What do you mean, what have we
been up to?'

'You both returned in a far different mood. Something
happened to change it; I want to know what.'

So he *had* heard them laughing. Nevertheless he had
no right questioning her. 'I think that what Greg and I
do is our own business,' she answered coolly. And let
him make of that what he would.

'Denial means that you're hiding something,' he declared, accusation now harsh in his tone, brows drawn
together fiercely.

Her eyes flashed defensively. 'You have a vile mind,
Hallam Lane.'

'I do not like the idea that you jumped out of my arms
and into my son's.'

'I didn't.'

'So tell me what you were doing.'

'Simply talking,' she retorted.

'What about? You and me?'

'Why would we do that?' she questioned sharply.

'Greg must be curious.'

'Maybe,' she answered with a shrug, 'but it's up to you to fill him in on all the sordid details. He got nothing from me.'

'He did not ask?'

'He mentioned it, yes,' she admitted with a faint shrug, 'but only to express his regret for observing me almost naked. And I can assure you right here and now that what happened earlier will never happen again, not in a hundred years.'

He looked solemn all of a sudden. 'Would it help if I apologised?'

'Not in the least,' she retorted. 'I wouldn't believe you were sincere, for one thing.'

'You shouldn't be so irresistible,' he growled. 'How is a man supposed to keep his hands off you?'

So he wasn't laying all the blame on her! Abby felt slightly appeased, and indeed felt a sudden, unexpected warmth steal through her, but she nevertheless still felt that he had treated her unfairly. 'Can I go now?' she asked.

'I just need one promise from you.'

Abby looked at him cautiously and warily. Now what was coming?

'Make sure you *do* keep your relationship with Greg strictly platonic,' he warned, 'He's far too young for you.'

Her eyes flashed with a sudden spurt of anger. 'I don't think I have anything to say to that, Mr Lane. I like your son, and I respect him, which is more than I can say for his father.' And with that she jumped to her feet, threw him one last furious glance, and then marched back into the house.

Hallam totally confused her. There was no foundation for such a warning. She and Greg had done nothing except talk and laugh and enjoy themselves. They were on holiday—a time when everyone let their hair down. Surely he could see that? Surely he didn't expect her to ignore his son for the next two weeks? That would be no fun at all.

Eventually she crawled into bed, but her mind was too active to allow sleep, and when morning came she felt as though she hadn't slept a wink, though possibly she had managed a couple of hours.

A shower refreshed her to a certain extent but she was conscious of the shadows beneath her eyes and the fatigue in her limbs. It seemed that ever since meeting Hallam she had had no sleep. He was a most disturbing man—in more ways than one!

She pulled on a jazzy silk shift, fixed her hair in a single plait, and went downstairs. She found the men outside. Hallam looked at her closely as she joined him and Greg smiled but said nothing. The table was set for breakfast and the sun had not yet reached the courtyard. It was warm but pleasant, without any of the humidity that was so uncomfortable during the main part of the day.

To her surprise—and her relief—Hallam acted as though nothing untoward had happened. He was cheerful and talkative and Abby began to feel a whole lot better. She took her lead from him and soon the three of them were chatting like old friends.

'I thought I'd show you something of the local countryside,' he said when they had finished eating, 'unless you have other ideas.'

'Not at all; I'd like that,' she answered immediately, both pleased and surprised by his suggestion. She hadn't expected this. 'I've never been to France before; I'd like to see as much as I can.'

Jaime came out to clear the table, announcing at the same time, 'You have a visitor, Hallam. Monsieur Duvall is here. He wants to—'

Before the French girl could finish Rod emerged from the shadows of the house, his eyes immediately seeking Abby's. A flicker of alarm ran through her; it looked as though her new-found peace was about to be shattered. She gave a faint smile of acknowledgement in return.

Hallam, catching the look, jumped to his feet, his eyes darkly savage, his brow breaking out into a thunderous frown. 'You're not welcome here, Duvall. Abby is my guest; she belongs to me.'

Rod looked unperturbed. 'Actually it's not Abby I've come to see, though I must admit I wish it was. She's gorgeous.'

Hallam's eyebrows grew into a furious straight line as he narrowed a questioning gaze at the younger man.

'No, sir,' went on Rod, 'I'm here to deliver an invitation from my parents. They're having a little get-together this evening and the three of you are invited.' Unfortunately he looked at Abby as he spoke.

A further flash of fury crossed Hallam's face. 'Thank your parents very much, but no thanks,' came his grating response.

Rod looked surprised by his refusal. 'They'll be hurt if you don't come. They said you always attend their parties, that a party without you is no party at all. Guess you've got yourself quite a reputation.'

Abby looked at Hallam curiously. What sort of a reputation? He had not given her the impression of being a party animal.

'Nevertheless I shall decline on this occasion,' answered Hallam coldly. 'I have already made plans for this evening.'

Abby was sure he hadn't, and when she caught Greg's eye she could see that this was the first he'd heard of it also.

'What plans, Father?' he asked. 'I think it's a splendid idea.'

'I do too,' she added. 'Will all your other neighbours be there, Rod? I'd like to meet them.'

'Half of France, I guess,' he said. 'My mother always does things in a big way.'

'Then we won't be missed,' snorted Hallam.

But Rod was insistent. 'My folks will be most insulted if you refuse. They'll think they've offended you in some way.'

Hallam looked at Rod and then he looked at Abby, as if wondering how much of this was because of her. But in the end, after a fierce battle with himself, he reluctantly gave in. 'We'll show our faces for a few minutes. Satisfied?'

Rod nodded and gave Abby a broad grin. 'See you this evening, then, beautiful one.' He seemed not to care that Hallam was watching and disapproving.

Abby felt uneasy at the thought that she could be the real reason why Rod had been so insistent, and when he disappeared and Hallam rounded on her she knew that he was of the same opinion.

CHAPTER NINE

'ROD DUVALL'S not to be trusted,' Hallam told Abby strongly once he was sure the other man had left the house. 'I don't want you associating with him.'

'How do you know?' she asked coldly, her eyes flashing a brilliant, belligerent green. How dared he try to tell her what she could or could not do?

'Because he's the type,' he answered impatiently. 'Can't you see that?'

'I saw that he was friendly and looked as though he'd be a great deal of fun,' she returned, her eyes still flashing her resentment.

'Fun!' He made the word sound as though it had several different meanings.

Abby glared. 'You're disgusting. First you say I have my sights set on Greg, and now you think I'm interested in Rod. What sort of a mind do you have, for heaven's sake? Only the other day you seemed to find it surprising that I'd had no steady boyfriends.'

Out of the corner of her eye she saw Greg give a start of surprise when she mentioned his name, and she wished now that she had not let her tongue run away with her. What must he be thinking?

Hallam too had seen his son's astonishment. 'You'd better leave us, Greg,' he said, and once they were alone he went on. 'I'd thank you, Sommers, not to talk like that in front of my son.'

Her chin firmed. 'If you hadn't made the accusation in the first place there would have been no need.' But she was nevertheless cross with herself; she wouldn't hurt Greg for anything. She felt deeply ashamed of her outburst. His face had been a picture of confusion when he'd left the room.

'That's beside the point.'

'Is it?' she questioned, eyes wide and filled with hostility. 'I don't think so. And, while we're on the subject of your son, I think you should have a talk with him about his future.'

Her abrupt change of subject caused a sudden fierce frown to scour his brow. 'Greg's future? What the hell are you talking about?'

'What he wants to do when he leaves university,' she said levelly. 'Let's say I got more out of him in the short time I've known him than you seem to have done in years.'

His frown deepened, his eyes even more menacing. 'You really have had some meaningful conversations, haven't you?' He looked deeply angry that she had got so close to his son in such a short space of time.

Abby shrugged. 'I cared enough to ask questions.'

'You're saying I don't?' he barked.

'No, not at all,' she answered quickly, knowing the folly of antagonising him too much. 'I know you love him, and Greg loves you, but he feels he's a disappointment to you and—I don't know—perhaps that's the reason he can't open his heart.'

Hallam was still frowning. 'He's always given the impression that he has no interest in anything. I've spoken to him about it. I cannot understand why he's talked to you and not to me.'

'I guess I have the knack of inviting confidences,' she

said softly. 'Listen to your son; I think you'll be surprised.' And, deciding enough had been said, she got up from the table.

'A word of warning about tonight,' he growled. 'We won't be staying long and I don't want Rod monopolising you. There will be plenty of other interesting people for you to talk to.'

'Don't try to run my life,' she flashed back irritably. 'I don't belong to you, Hallam Lane, not by any stretch of the imagination. I'll talk to whom I like.'

After that she doubted whether they would be going out to see the sights. It hadn't taken much to ruin things again. But Hallam surprised her by declaring they would be leaving in a few minutes.

'It's still on, then?' she could not help asking.

He shot her a look of surprise. 'Is there any reason why it shouldn't be?'

She shrugged. 'I thought maybe you wouldn't feel inclined to go out after…' Her voice faltered.

'After Duvall's unfortunate visit, you mean?' he asked crisply.

She nodded.

'I have no intention of letting someone like him ruin my day,' he told her. 'It's unfortunate enough that we have to be back in order to attend his parents' get-together. They usually give more notice than this.'

Abby was curious. 'Don't you like socialising with your neighbours?'

'I used to,' he admitted. 'I've been to many of their parties, but things change.'

Like the Duvalls' son appearing on the scene, thought Abby bitterly. But she decided to say no more and hurried to her room, where she brushed her teeth, picked up her bag and was back downstairs in no time at all.

She had assumed that Greg would be going with them and was surprised and a little perturbed when Hallam settled her into his smart red sports car and turned the key in the ignition with no sight of his son.

She looked at him sharply. 'Where's Greg?' she asked, frowning.

'He's not coming,' came the short response.

'But why?' Abby's disapproval showed in her voice. 'It's unfair to leave him here alone.' She swung her door open, and, uncaring whether he got the wrong idea or not, she said, 'If Greg's not coming then you can count me out as well.' And she got out of the car.

Hallam's hiss of anger was loud. 'Come back here, Sommers!' he barked. 'You're making an utter fool of yourself.'

'Am I?' she charged, turning round to face him. 'I don't think so.'

He leapt out of the car also and they faced each other across its gleaming body. 'Is it Greg or me you want to go out with?' he rasped.

Her eyes met his coldly, but she could not stem the sudden rapid beat of her heart. 'Both, as a matter of fact,' she told him. 'There's nothing here for Greg to do. He'll be bored out of his mind.'

'Really?' Dark brows rose. 'As a matter of fact it was his decision to stay at home.'

Abby swallowed. 'It was?'

'That's right, so don't you think you'd better sit in again so that we can get going?'

'But why doesn't he want to come?' she persisted. 'Or did you put the idea into his mind that he wouldn't be welcome?' she added suspiciously.

'Of course I didn't.' His tone was sharply condemning. 'But we had a long talk last night after you'd gone to bed. I needed to clear up a few things.'

Like her racing naked out of his room, thought Abby wryly, wondering how he had explained that to his son, though she knew she dared not ask.

'And he said then that he wouldn't be coming with us,' he informed her.

Abby wondered if it was Greg's way of throwing them together—in the hope that they would overcome their differences. And, if so, what had he thought of her earlier statement? She hoped to goodness he wouldn't believe that she was interested in him romantically. That really would disrupt the holiday.

Reluctantly she climbed back into the car and once they were away from the villa, once they were out in the open countryside with its perfect, perfect light, Abby forgot her dissatisfaction and was entranced. She wished she had remembered to bring her camera with her; she wished she could record all this on film.

Hallam proved to be surprisingly good company. He pointed out places of interest, stopped willingly and patiently when she wanted to explore any particular village or church, and she wondered why he couldn't be like this all the time.

He was actually fun to be with today, a perfect companion, an expert guide, and although she still felt a strong awareness she was able to hide it while he was in this convivial mood.

They ended up having lunch at a quayside café in nearby St Tropez, where they watched the rich and the perhaps not so famous sipping martinis on their yacht decks. Hallam told her that most of the truly famous people who had permanent homes here departed during the summer when the tourists came.

For a couple of hours they sat in the shade of the café awning, drinking coffee and talking about anything and everything. He told her about his childhood, the fact that his father had suffered ill health for many, many years and had been unable to work, that he had dearly wanted to go to university but had got himself a job instead in order to make his parents' life more comfortable, and that he had always been determined to make something of his life, education or not.

'Are your parents still alive?' she asked softly. She understood now why Greg had said that Hallam thought making money was important.

'No,' he admitted sadly. 'My father died ten years ago, and my mother shortly afterwards from a broken heart.' His lips twisted, his eyes became shadowed. 'They were very devoted to each other.'

'I'm sorry,' she said.

When they eventually arrived back at the villa after a long and surprisingly happy day, it was to find Greg missing and a message left with Jaime to say that he had gone out with Rod on *Fast Lady*.

Hallam did not look very pleased but he did not explode into fury as Abby half expected. The ban on going out with Rod obviously only applied to herself.

The pool tempted her and she ran upstairs to pull on a swimsuit. Hallam was in it before her and they spent the next half-hour slipping in and out of the water like seals. Abby felt happier than she had since arriving and she hoped it boded well for the rest of the holiday.

When they accidentally surfaced within inches of each other he took one dark, desperate look at her and lifted her by the waist as high as he could, then let her slide slowly and sensuously down the silken hardness of his body, his movements controlled, his powerful muscles hardly rippling as he took her full weight.

It was highly erotic and aroused sensations that had been simmering all day, and when he kissed her Abby was as ready for him as he was for her. As if the bones in their bodies had melted they both slid slowly beneath the surface still kissing, rising only to take desperate gulps of air before claiming each other's mouths again and sinking to their watery paradise.

The experience was new and profoundly exciting and when his hands slowly and tormentingly caressed her aching breasts, when they slid with excruciating slowness from her slender waist to her gently rounded hips and buttocks, when he traced every inch of her as though he were a blind man trying to commit her shape to memory, Abby had no thought to stop him; indeed her own hands were unashamedly exploring him too.

When a groan was dragged from him, when he suddenly pulled her even closer, jamming her hard against him, Abby felt as though she was about to go crazy. Every pulse in her body worked overtime, her heart slammed against her ribcage, her head spun, and she urged her hips forward, grinding herself against him, feeling sure that if they'd had enough air in their lungs he would have made love to her right there beneath the water.

As it was, their need for air was much greater, and they pushed themselves to the surface, still entwined in each other's arms, just as Greg approached the pool, prepared to join them. He looked faintly surprised to see them locked together, so obviously enjoying themselves together, and then he grinned and Abby could almost see him congratulating himself. 'Not intruding, am I?'

'You could have chosen your moment better,'

growled Hallam, trying to look fierce but failing. And in an undertone to Abby he muttered, 'This is something I most definitely intend finishing later.'

She was deliriously happy that for once he had not thought better of it and the three of them cavorted and played in the water for another good quarter of an hour. Abby hoped, most fervently, that Rod would not do or say anything this evening to ruin the sudden rapport between her and Hallam. She almost wished they weren't going.

When she finally announced that she'd had enough and was going to take a shower she half expected Hallam to follow; instead he remained behind with his son and from the balcony Abby saw them deep in conversation. She smiled and headed for the bathroom.

Afterwards, clad in nothing more than a short peach satin robe, Abby threw herself down on the bed to reflect on the events of the day—and made a startling discovery! Harriet had been right after all. *She was in love with Hallam Lane.*

This was no physical need; it was a deep-seated emotional one. It went right into her very soul, and it both thrilled and dismayed her at the same time. She could hope and pray that Hallam felt the same, but she could not make it happen, and indeed all indications were that he desired her body and nothing else.

Confusion reigned in her mind and it was at this precise moment that Hallam appeared in the open balcony doorway. He was freshly showered and wore nothing more than a white towel around his loins. 'Waiting for me?' he growled softly, and as he loped towards the bed he dropped the towel.

Abby's body went into panic. Despite loving him she was not ready to make such a commitment. It would be foolish, fatal, insane! She would regret it for the rest of her life.

She quickly sat up. 'I was just about to get ready for the Duvalls' party,' she murmured, dismayed at the huskiness of her tone, and even more distraught by the impact of his finely honed male body on her hormones. He was so magnificent that she found it difficult to drag her eyes from him.

'There's plenty of time for that,' he told her firmly, and, not in the least self-conscious about his nudity, Hallam sat on the edge of the bed and gently pushed her back down again. Abby, to her own surprise, let him, though some of her confusion must have shown on her face because he frowned and said, 'Not having a change of heart, are you, Sommers?'

It was his use of her surname that did it. She couldn't make love to a man who called her Sommers, despite the vortex of sensations that churned inside her. She jerked herself up again, eyes flashing fire now. 'As a matter of fact, yes, I am. I think the sun must have got to me earlier.'

But before she could jump off the bed his hands shot forward and imprisoned her wrists. 'I don't think so, my beautiful one.' His tone was seductively low, sending further tremors of excitement down her spine. 'I think you were following the dictates of your body.' And his thumbs began a slow, erotic, circular stroke on her pulses.

If he had said the dictates of her heart, she might have had second thoughts, might even have believed that his heart was involved too. But he was making it absolutely clear that he wanted nothing more from her than a brief affair, a holiday romance; call it what you like, it all amounted to the same thing.

'My body would never let me get involved with a swine like you,' she said strongly, frightened now of how much she had given away, frightened also of what he was doing to her. If only he were dressed; if only they weren't on the bed; if only...

'My, my, we certainly are in a fighting mood, aren't we?' Strong brows rose questioningly. 'What ever's happened to cause this change in such a remarkably short space of time?'

Abby lifted her chin and tried to look scornful. 'Let's say I came to my senses.' She wished he would let her go, wished her pulses did not throb so erratically—he must surely feel them! And her heart felt as though it was trying to leap out of her breast.

'Still afraid of letting a man into your bourgeois little life?' he taunted.

'Of course not. I've never been afraid,' she retorted haughtily, though she was careful not to let her eyes meet his. 'I've simply never met the right man.'

'Perhaps you've never let one near enough to find out.' His hand moved deftly to slip the knot in her belt, to slide audaciously inside the peach satin garment, and to cup possessively the soft contour of a breast. 'I have a feeling that I've got closer than anyone,' he murmured, his voice growing deeper and softer and infinitely persuasive. 'And you cannot say that you don't like it. You give yourself away every time.'

Abby drew in a swift breath as she experienced a moment of quivering shock. It had happened so quickly and unexpectedly that she had not been able to stop him, and now it was too late! Already immense excitement raced from throat to groin; every limb tingled and quivered in anticipation. One touch, she thought in despair, and she was his to do with as he liked. Her love had robbed her of all sane reasoning.

She closed her eyes, trying to blot out this man who was turning her world upside down, who was creating sensations inside her that should never be allowed. It was impossible. His touch triggered every nerve-end. She trembled beneath his touch. He was right—she did give herself away.

Hallam's hand came up to palm the back of her head, to drive her mouth insistently against his. His tongue found its eager way into her mouth and Abby made no attempt to stop him.

Her robe slipped from her shoulders, though whether it had a helping hand from Hallam she could not be sure. Whatever, she made only a slight demur when he pressed her back down against the pillows, her protest turning to a cry of exquisite pleasure when he sucked her peaked nipple into his mouth.

She knew that she ought to be fighting him off, she ought not to be allowing this invasion of her senses. But instead her body flowered beneath his touch, and her hands curved around him to feel the smooth skin of his back and trace the strong muscle and sinew beneath.

Hallam lifted his head to look at her, his hungry eyes devouring her exposed body slow, torturous inch by slow, torturous inch, and then he kissed her again, his lips tracing exquisite lines from the tip of her aching breasts to the silken smoothness of her inner thighs, not missing one inch of her delicately perfumed skin.

Desire mounted in Abby like a volcano about to erupt and although she knew it was insanity she could not summon up the energy to roll off the bed and call a halt. Instead she wriggled beneath him with sheer, unadulter-ated pleasure, trying to tell herself that she could put a stop to it if she wanted, while knowing that she could do nothing of the sort.

She was completely under his spell now, she was his to do with as he liked, and if that meant he was going to take her all the way then she could do nothing to stop him. She loved this man unreservedly, and love, she had discovered, had a way of making the body weak, the mind helpless.

When he lay over her, when he thrust his thigh between hers, nudging her legs wide, Abby's body involuntarily arched, her arms going around him once more, her nails digging into his fine flesh.

'Father! Father!' Greg's urgent voice from the courtyard below drummed into their consciousness.

Hallam groaned. 'Let's ignore him.'

But his son called again more loudly and even more urgently and he was forced to lift himself off her. 'Stay there, whatever you do,' he said throatily, pausing to drop a kiss on each aching breast before crossing to the balcony.

Abby wrapped her arms around herself, savouring the feeling of excitement and anticipation and deep, deep hunger that Hallam had aroused in her, that danced and sang and set her whole body on fire. Because she irrevocably loved this man none of it felt wrong—even though she was aware of the limitations of his feelings. Better this than nothing at all, she told herself.

Lord, her body felt ravaged already, quivering and unusually heavy, her hips contracting with tiny involuntary movements, her swollen breasts desperately aching, longing for his return. 'Please hurry, Hallam,' she whispered.

So wrapped up was she in her own needs, in the feelings that were engulfing her that she had not listened to his conversation with Greg and was distraught when he suddenly announced that he had to leave.

'What's wrong?' she asked, wide-eyed, a sudden chill sweeping over her.

'Jaime tripped out by the pool,' he answered briefly. 'She may have broken her ankle; I need to take her to hospital.'

Immediately Abby was fully alert, her own needs forgotten. 'I'll come with you.'

'There's no need,' he said at once. 'You and Greg carry on and go to the Duvalls if I'm not back. I'll meet you there.'

'Perhaps we should not go at all?' She would much rather have lain here and waited for him. She could have curled up and savoured each moment, dreamt of the sweet torment to come.

'A promise is a promise,' he said wryly, 'much as I'd like to get out of it.' And on a much thicker, lower note he added, 'Just make sure you keep yourself for me.' His mouth captured hers for a few thudding seconds, and then he had gone silently to his room. All that remained to remind her that he'd been was the towel which had earlier draped the most intimate part of his anatomy.

Abby could so easily have felt relief, been glad of this second reprieve; instead frustration was uppermost. For several minutes she lay there, her body still throbbing and experiencing mind-defying sensations. Why had this happened now?

When she finally managed to drag herself off the bed and begin her preparations for the party, it occurred to her that Hallam could have used Jaime's accident as an excuse for neither of them to go. Considering he had never wanted to accept in the first place, it would have been the perfect get-out. They would have got together again so much sooner. Now she had goodness knew how long to wait. Could her body bear it?

Abby chose to wear a black dress that was several years old but had timeless elegance none the less; sleeveless, scoop-necked, skimming the knee, its only pretence to embellishment was a scalloped line of pearls around the hem. She had popped it into her suitcase on an impulse and now was glad that she had because nothing else she had brought with her was suitable for the occasion.

Pearl earrings and a three-stranded pearl choker completed the ensemble and she stood back to study the effect in the full-length, white-framed mirror.

With her hair loose and a glow to her face that had everything to do with Hallam she knew that she looked nearer the eighteen years he sometimes accused her of seeming. She smiled happily, pleased with her appearance. If this was what love did then she was all for it. When she appeared downstairs Greg was every bit as impressed as she hoped his parent would be.

'I'm sorry I had to drag my father away from you,' he said as they set out on the short walk to the Duvalls' villa.

Abby shook her head. 'Don't apologise. It couldn't be helped. I only hope Jaime isn't seriously hurt. What happened exactly?'

'She tripped over a lounger,' he explained. 'She was admiring the geraniums on the balcony instead of watching where she was going.'

Or, more likely, the maid had known that Hallam was in her room and that was why she had been looking up! Abby felt as guilty as if the accident had been her fault.

'I'm glad that you and my father are—er—friends.' Greg dismissed the incident from his mind.

'Don't read too much into it,' she warned.

He kicked a stone. 'I think he likes you a lot, despite the way he treated you in the beginning.'

'I'm not so sure,' said Abby. 'I actually don't think it will last.'

Greg frowned. 'Forgive me for saying this, Abby, but you don't give the impression that you'd sleep around with someone you didn't love.'

Abby felt swift colour blaze across her cheeks and she turned to look at the ocean, not wanting Hallam's son to see her guilt. He couldn't have known that they'd been in bed together, could he?

'*Do* you love my father?' he asked, clearly not willing to give up the subject.

She drew in an unsteady breath and knew she could not lie. 'I guess so, but it must be our secret, Greg. I don't want him to know.'

The young man frowned. 'But why? Surely if you love a person you tell them?'

If only it was that easy, she thought. 'Because—because he doesn't return my feelings,' she said quickly. 'I think I'm simply a diversion for the duration of the holiday. He didn't want me here in the first place, if you remember.'

'I think you're wrong,' said Greg. 'My father wouldn't do that to you. And as for him saying that you are interested in *me* well, I soon put him right on that score.'

'I guess he just didn't like to see us getting on so well together,' said Abby, smiling, pleased with his sensible attitude. 'Not when he and I were always arguing. I'm sorry I blurted it out like that, though; he just made me so angry.'

'So long as we're still friends I don't care.'

'Of course we're friends, Greg.'

The Duvalls' villa was every bit as grand as Hallam's, with large, spacious, airy rooms, priceless paintings on the walls and expensive *objets d'art* everywhere. The colour scheme was bizarre, with bright, gaudy colours that were a complete mismatch. Nevertheless, it had an overwhelming sense of homeliness which, she discovered, came from Rita Duvall, who was plump and jolly and had no airs and graces whatsoever despite their considerable wealth. Frank, her husband, a retired financier, was a down-to-earth person also and Abby took to them immediately.

Rita naturally enquired why Hallam wasn't with them and was extremely concerned when she heard about Jaime's accident.

Abby and Greg were the first people to arrive and Rod took it upon himself to give her a guided tour of the house. 'God, but you look beautiful tonight,' he enthused. 'Not that you don't always but there's an extra special glow about you. I sincerely hope it was the thought of seeing me.'

Abby laughed. 'But of course.'

'With a bit of luck we'll be able to sneak away later and have some fun of our own. I don't mind telling you that I'm glad Hallam hasn't come. Considering he means nothing to you, he's far too protective for my peace of mind.'

'He'll be here later,' Abby reminded him.

'A lot later, I hope.' He tucked his arm around her and led her from room to room, not really giving her the opportunity to see anything, but keeping up a steady stream of compliments and expressing his desire to see a lot more of her in the days to come.

When an upstairs door burst open just as they were

walking past it and a vivacious, dark-haired girl in an emerald dress dashed out he introduced her as his sister. 'Vicki, this is Abby; she's staying with Hallam Lane. Abby—Victoria, my baby sister.'

'Less of the baby,' the girl tossed at him fiercely. 'I shall be twenty next month.'

'And don't you keep reminding us.'

'I didn't know Hallam was back in France. Why didn't anyone tell me?' Vicki gave Abby a long, deliberate stare that was less than friendly and seemed to be asking whether she was his girlfriend.

'There's a lot you don't know, little girl,' Rod taunted deliberately.

'Where is he? Is he downstairs?' The girl was already running in that direction.

'Afraid not, Vicki,' he called after her, laughter in his voice. 'He won't be here until later—much later—if at all.'

The girl skidded to a halt and looked back at him. 'You're lying.'

Rod shrugged. 'Ask Abby if you don't believe me.'

'It's true,' said Abby. 'He's had to take Jaime to hospital.'

'Why? What's wrong with her?' the girl questioned abruptly.

'She had a fall; nothing serious.'

'Then he will be here,' she cried, and continued on her way.

'My baby sister has a crush on the omnipotent Hallam Lane,' Rod remarked drily. 'Don't take any notice of her. Here's my room; care to see inside?'

Abby was not listening; she was thinking about Vicki and Hallam and wondering if he had ever encouraged the girl. It was not a thought that pleased her; Vicki was far too young.

'You haven't answered my question,' said Rod urgently, shaking her arm as he did so. 'Are you all right? You've gone very pale.'

'I'm fine,' said Abby. 'It's just the heat; I'm not used to it. What was your question?'

'I wondered if you'd like to see my room?' he repeated with a grin. And there was a wealth of meaning behind his words.

Abby shook her head. 'I don't think so.'

He shrugged easily. 'Of course you're right. It would look odd if we went missing just yet. We'll save that pleasure for later.'

It would be fatal to give him any wrong impression, thought Abby; best to establish the ground rules now.

'You're funny and entertaining and easy to get on with,' she said, 'but, much as I like you, I don't want to get involved.'

He looked disappointed, slapping a hand to his chest. 'My Greek goddess has turned me down; I'm mortally wounded.'

'And you're a liar to boot,' she returned with a laugh. 'Let's go back downstairs.'

'I'd like you to tell me one thing before we do.' He was suddenly serious—at least, as serious as he could be. 'You said Hallam wasn't interested in you but I know what I saw on the cliff top. Is he the person responsible for your aura of happiness?'

Abby could not lie. She grimaced guiltily. 'I'm afraid so, though I'm not sure whether anything will come of it.'

'And was it because of what I said about my little

sister having a crush on him that made you go deathly pale just now?'

He was too astute by far, despite the comic act he put on. But this time she was admitting nothing. 'Of course not.'

He lifted his shoulders and gave a rueful smile. 'Whatever the lady says. It would appear I've missed out again. Never mind; we'll enjoy ourselves while we can. I think I hear others arriving; best get down and introduce you. A new face is always welcome. You'll find yourself the centre of attention.'

As the evening progressed Abby found herself watching and waiting for Hallam. He was away much longer than she had expected and she could not help wondering whether Jaime herself was detaining him, making the most of the situation. Perhaps they were already back home and she was insisting that he keep her company. Either that or she was being detained in hospital and insisting that Hallam stay with her.

Abby dismissed the thoughts immediately as unworthy. Jealousy had a way of interpreting situations in entirely the wrong way. The maid was obviously undergoing treatment and Hallam was waiting to make sure she was all right. It was that simple.

'How long have you known Hallam?'

She was snapped out of her thoughts by Rod's young sister appearing at her side. Vicki had been watching her all evening, Abby was well aware of that, but she had not actually spoken to her until this moment.

'A few months,' she answered, though in truth the actual number of times they had met prior to coming out here could be no more than half a dozen.

'He's never brought a girlfriend to his villa before. Are you special to him?' Victoria had huge brown eyes that were long-lashed and extremely beautiful, a tiny tip-tilted nose, and pouting red lips. She was not very tall—about five feet four—but in her spiky high heels she was almost the same height as Abby. Her chin was high at this moment, her eyes bright and belligerent, as if saying, Why should he bring you?

Abby was not quite sure how to answer Vicki's question. She would like to be special to Hallam, but was she? Only he knew the answer to that. 'Our relationship is developing,' she said finally.

'And what is that supposed to mean?' queried the girl sharply. 'Is he your lover?'

The blunt question startled Abby and she looked at Vicki in surprise. 'I hardly think that's the sort of thing you should be asking a complete stranger.'

Vicki tossed her head. 'I want to know.' The girl had astounding self-confidence.

'Why?' asked Abby. 'Because you fancy him yourself?' She looked directly into the girl's eyes as she spoke.

'How do you know that?' came the instant, flaring response. 'Has my brother been talking? God, I hate him. He's always interfering in my life.'

Abby tried to protect Rod without actually lying. 'It's obvious from the way you're questioning me that you have some feelings for Hallam,' she said. 'Don't you think he's a little old for you?'

'I like older men,' cried the dark-haired girl peevishly. 'Age has nothing to do with it if two people love each other.'

Abby's heart felt as though it had been crushed. 'Hallam loves you—is that what you're saying?'

'Yes,' answered Vicki assuredly.

'He's told you this?'

A tiny shrug. 'Not in so many words, but actions speak louder, don't they?'

So he had made advances towards her! Bile rose in Abby's throat and almost gagged her. Lord, there must be something like a twenty-year age gap between them. What could Hallam be thinking of? And he'd had the gall to accuse her of making a play for Greg.

The nerves that tightened her stomach now were for an entirely different reason. Gone was desire, replaced by instant repulsion, and it was suddenly crystal-clear why he hadn't wanted to come to this party—it wasn't because of Rod, it was because he did not want her and Vicki to meet!

CHAPTER TEN

'I EXPECT Hallam didn't realise I was here,' trilled Vicki, apparently unaware of the bombshell she had dropped, 'or he'd have been round before now. I hope he hurries up.'

Abby had to get away; she couldn't stand here listening to this girl gushing over Hallam. 'Excuse me,' she said, smiling with difficulty, 'I need to get another drink.' Another drink meant a tonic water, which is what she had been on all evening, although she had to confess that at this moment she felt like something a whole lot stronger. She wanted to get drunk; she wanted oblivion.

She felt Vicki's eyes stabbing her back as she walked away and after her glass had been refilled by one of the smiling topless male waiters whom Rita and Frank had hired for the occasion she went outside onto the terrace and drank in great breaths of fresh air.

Like Hallam's it had terrific views of the ocean below. It was strung with coloured lights and piped music was softly playing. Couples danced in intimate clinches but she managed to find a quiet corner where she could be alone with her thoughts. She wished now that she hadn't come, that she had sat at home and waited for Hallam. She didn't want to know about Vicki.

Her peace was soon shattered. Hardly had she begun thinking about Vicki's devastating declaration and the mind-blowing effect it was having on her than Rod joined her. 'So here you are,' he said cheerfully. 'I wondered where you had got to. The noise too much, eh?'

'Something like that,' she admitted, wondering why people were always so insensitive to others' needs. Couldn't he see that she wanted to be alone?

'I saw you having an intent conversation with my kid sister,' he said, standing beside her so that they could watch the restless ocean together. 'What was that all about? Not making a nuisance of herself, was she?'

The corner of Abby's mouth lifted and she kept her tone deliberately light. It wouldn't do to let him know how the girl had hurt her. 'She wanted to know what the position is between Hallam and myself.'

'I guessed as much,' he said matter-of-factly. 'She seems to think she has a prior claim on him. Apparently he nearly always holidays here alone and the little brat, needless to say, makes a beeline for him. I wouldn't worry if I were you; there's nothing in it.'

'How do you know?'

'Because my parents would never allow it, for one thing,' he retorted, his voice full of conviction. 'He's much too old for her.'

Did that really make any difference? she wondered. 'Don't they know that she has a—crush on him?'

'Of course,' he agreed easily, 'but they see it as a passing phase, which is what it is, Abby, darling. She's at the stage where she thinks she's in love with every available man.'

'She hinted that they were lovers.'

For just an instant shock widened Rod's blue eyes. Then he relaxed and smiled. 'Most definitely wishful thinking on her part. I wouldn't believe a word she says. He's a trusted friend of my parents; he would never do that to their daughter.'

Abby was not so sure. She had firsthand evidence that Hallam Lane had no qualms about making love to a woman he did not love.

It was almost eleven when Hallam finally turned up—Abby had been thinking for over an hour now of suggesting to Greg that they go home. Their 'few minutes' at the party had turned into three hours.

As soon as she saw him her heart flipped and her pulses set off on a determined path all of their own—despite what she had just discovered!

His eyes were searching the crowd of laughing, talking people; for her, she hoped—or was it Vicki? Suddenly the girl appeared at his side, tugging his arm, and when he looked down there was a look of tenderness on his face that told all.

He picked the tiny girl up by the waist and swung her round and she planted a kiss fairly and squarely on his lips. There was open adoration here and Abby could not watch any longer.

She headed for the terrace again and Rod was close behind her. 'It's not what you think, my Titian-haired goddess. My dearest sister is doing all the running; he can hardly ignore her.'

But he didn't have to greet her so enthusiastically. 'Dance with me, Rod,' she said on a frantic note.

'My pleasure, dear heart.' The music playing over the loudspeakers was a slow, seductive waltz, and Abby allowed herself to be held close, wrapping her arms around Rod, resting her head on his shoulder and closing her eyes, as if by so doing she could shut out Hallam and the rest of the world as well.

'This must be my lucky day,' murmured Rod, his arms tightening about her. 'Maybe I have something to thank my sister for after all.'

'Don't get any ideas,' she said tartly.

'As if I would,' he answered.

The piece of music finished and another began and still Abby kept herself hidden in Rod's arms, until a harsh voice sounded in her ear.

'Excuse me, I think this lady's mine.'

Rod did not immediately let her go, his arm remaining proprietarily around her shoulders as they half parted to acknowledge Hallam. 'Maybe Abby should decide for herself,' he said, a note of challenge in his voice which surprised her. She had not expected Rod to be so protective.

Hallam's dark eyes were as hard as polished jet as they fixed accusingly on her face. 'Well, Abby?'

In his present condemning mood she knew that it would be best all round if she joined him, that no good purpose would be served by refusing. All it would do was cause an ugly scene, and that was something she didn't really want, especially as she was a stranger in their midst. It wouldn't be fair on the Duvalls, for one thing.

But she could not forget the sight of him and Vicki together—where was the girl now?—and she contrarily gave Rod a warm kiss on the lips before extracting herself from his embrace. 'Save a dance for me later,' she said with false gaiety.

'There will be no later,' came Hallam's grim retort. 'We're going home.'

'But you've only just got here,' she protested frowningly.

'As if you noticed,' he ground out, his hand bruising as he frogmarched her away. 'Been having a good time, have you, Sommers?'

'Damn you!' she riposted.

'Been monopolising Rod Duvall all evening?' he sneered. 'Been offering him your body the same as you did me?'

Abby could not believe that she was hearing these things and a slow anger began to burn inside her. She wrenched herself free and stood facing him. 'I don't think *you* have any right to talk.'

A harsh frown cut deep furrows in his brow. 'And what is that supposed to mean?' His lips were tight and thin, his eyes no more that glittering slits.

'It means that I know all about your little *affair* with Rod's sister,' she threw at him, 'and I think it stinks; you're old enough to be her father.'

Hallam's jaw tightened. 'Who's been telling tales?' he asked quietly.

She shrugged, noting painfully that he did not deny it. 'I didn't need to hear it from anyone; I saw it with my own eyes when she greeted you. And I saw the way you treated her, so don't try to get out of it. I'm surprised she's let you out of her sight; she's been looking for you all evening.'

'Victoria means nothing to me,' he declared firmly and dismissively.

Abby's eyes flashed. 'You mean you've simply taken advantage of her innocent young body? Is she the reason you didn't want to come to this party? You were worried in case she said something that might embarrass you? Is that it?'

'You're making a mistake, Sommers,' he warned, his voice bitingly cold.

'Am I?' she demanded, her tone equally icy. 'I don't think so. You see, Vicki's already told me everything that's been going on between you. We had quite an eye-opening conversation.'

'She is at an impressionable age; she makes things up,' he said easily.

'You would say that, wouldn't you?' she retorted. What had happened to the beautiful evening? Where was the harmony between them? Sadly she knew now that they would never regain those precious few minutes when she had soared with the eagles and her whole future had looked rosy.

Her love would be forced to die a natural death—if it ever did. Her feelings for Hallam were so strong that she was sure she would carry them with her for the rest of her life.

'It happens to be the truth,' he declared. 'Where's Greg? I'll tell him we're leaving.'

Neither or them could see him and Hallam seemed to think this was something else that was her fault. 'I suppose you've been so intent on Rod Duvall that you haven't thought to keep my son company.'

'You swine!' she spat. 'You know nothing.' And suddenly she spotted Greg on the far side of the room—and who should be wrapped in his arms but the beautiful Victoria Duvall? 'There's your son,' she said. 'And just look who's making a meal of him.'

She watched Hallam's face closely as his eyes sought out and found Greg, but he kept his feelings well hidden; there was no sign that he was disturbed by the two of them together. Nevertheless Abby did see the flickering of a muscle in his jaw.

'Are you going to split them up?' she asked demurely. 'It can't be very nice seeing your baby girlfriend in the arms of your son.' Sarcasm was not normally a part of Abby's nature but the circumstances were such that the words came out before she had given any thought to them.

'Don't move from this spot,' said Hallam through clenched teeth, adding warningly, 'And if Duvall dares so much as to look at you again I won't be responsible for my actions. Is that clear?'

'You don't own me, Hallam,' she retorted, finding it extremely difficult to accept that he was saying these things.

As he made his way across the room—a slow progress because many people stopped to have a word with him—she realised that she did not want to go back to the villa with Hallam Lane—not while he was in this mood. All night long she had looked forward to his return, to going to bed with him, to making love for hour upon hour. And now, with his irrational anger, he had spoilt everything. There was no hope any more.

A further disquieting thought struck her. What if he still planned to make love to her, regardless? What if he forced himself on her? A cold trickle ran down her spine. This was something she could not stomach. Not at any cost. Without stopping to think where she was going Abby ran out of the party.

The beach seemed the best place to sit and think and be alone, and, Lord, did she need to think. So much had happened in the short time she'd been in France, the most surprising thing being that she had fallen in love with Hallam Lane. And now that love was doomed. Her first love—at the age of twenty-nine!—and most probably her last. What had she done to deserve this?

She took off her heeled sandals at the top of the Duvalls' steps—wooden and well-used, the same as Hallam's—and then ran down as fast as her legs would carry her. It was a wonder she hadn't fallen, thought Abby when she finally reached the bottom. That would have been an even bigger catastrophe. What if she had ended up in the same hospital as Jaime? She giggled at the thought and then asked herself what she was laughing at.

She marched angrily along the beach, her strides long, her back straight. She ought never to have let Hallam make love to her in the first place. She ought never to have kissed him. She ought never to have allowed him even to touch her. In fact she ought not to have come here. She had only herself to blame for what had happened.

When she reached the rocks that skirted the far reaches of the bay Abby stepped nimbly from one to another until she was at their outermost point, almost overhanging the whispering waters of the Mediterranean. Finally she sat down and hugged her knees. The sky was a beautiful inky black, lit only by the fullness of a silver moon which shimmered over the sea's gently undulating surface.

It was so beautiful, and yet there was such discord in her mind and her heart. It was a cruel act of fate for her to fall in love and then discover that no good could ever come of it. Perhaps, if he hadn't accused her of throwing herself at Rod, and if she hadn't seen him with Victoria, then things might have been different. Perhaps...

There was no hope now, though. She felt furious when she recalled how he had picked Vicki up and kissed her so warmly. It had been proof enough of the way he felt about her. He could deny it however much he liked but she had seen with her own eyes how it was between them. In an abrupt gesture of disgust she got to her feet again.

But anger made her careless; quite how it happened Abby did not know, but somehow she missed her footing, her toe slipped between two rocks and she pitched forward. With a cry that rent the air she fell headlong into the deep waters below.

Everything happened in slow motion. She was not afraid of the water; Greg had told her that he often dived off these rocks and that it was perfectly safe. But she was close in to the rock face, much too close, and she felt a sudden excruciating pain as she caught her head a glancing blow. All went black.

It was Hallam's voice that she heard next, floating in and out of her consciousness, so faint that she could hardly hear him. 'Abby, Abby, can you hear me? Abby, don't die on me. I love you. Abby, I love you.'

Hallam loved her! *Hallam loved her!* Abby struggled to surface from the heavy blackness that was weighing her down. But as she did so the pain in her head grew unbearable and all she wanted to do was lie still and go back to sleep and dream this beautiful dream where Hallam was declaring that he loved her.

This was real. This was no dream. He *was* here! Had he spoken those words? She tried desperately hard to open her eyes but it was as though a great weight were holding her lids down and it took an age and a tremendous amount of will-power to force them apart.

She could just about make out Hallam's hazy shape, the big build of him hunched over her, his worried expression. She made an effort to smile, albeit weakly.

'Thank God,' he breathed fervently, and some of the worry lines faded. 'Thank God. For a moment there I thought that you—'

'My head,' she husked, wincing again as she tried to move.

'We must get you back to the house,' he said, suddenly matter-of-fact. 'You have a nasty gash on your head but I've checked and you appear to have no broken bones so I'm going to carry you, Abby. Is that all right? I do know what I'm doing, I promise you. I did an extensive first-aid course many years ago.'

'Yes,' she whispered. 'Do whatever you have to.' All she wanted was to be made comfortable, for this pain to go away.

Abby had only the faintest awareness of the journey up the steep steps, and of Hallam stripping off her wet clothes and wrapping her in a blanket. He was careful and gentle and she had an overwhelming sense of being loved. Had he said that, or had she dreamt it? She could not quite remember. It actually hurt to think and she preferred to sleep. But somewhere in the back of her mind the thought would not go away.

An ambulance arrived and she was taken to hospital, where her head was X-rayed, her wound cleaned and stitched, and then she was put into a narrow bed with crisp white sheets in a small private room. Hallam never left her side, not for one single second.

How many hours passed Abby did not know, but the room was flooded with sunlight when she next opened her eyes, and the bright light hurt. She blinked and squinted and held her hand over her eyes and Hallam immediately got up and lowered the blinds.

'How are you feeling?' He looked and sounded anxious as he sat back down beside the bed and took her hand between his.

'All right, I think,' she whispered.

'Does your head still hurt?'

'Yes, but not so much.'

'Are you up to talking?'

'Maybe, for a little while,' she answered faintly. She wanted to find out whether she had been dreaming when she'd heard him say he loved her, whether it had all been a figment of her imagination or whether it was for real. Despite the painkillers which made her feel light-headed and lethargic her body was reacting to his, to his nearness, to his touch, to the look of distress in his eyes.

'I had no right speaking to you the way I did,' he said. 'The trouble was, I just saw red when I saw the way Rod Duvall was holding you, the way you were snuggled up to him. I imagined you'd been together all evening and I couldn't handle it, not after what had happened between us only hours earlier.'

Abby did not speak, but just lay and listened and looked at him.

'I began to think all sorts of things about you—that maybe you'd lied and there had been other men. I thought that perhaps I was one of a crowd. I couldn't take it, Abby.'

Still she remained silent.

'I guess you'll want to go home now?'

'I guess I will,' she said quietly. 'How's Jaime?' She must definitely have imagined his declaration of love, for there was no word of it now. A terrible sadness filled her.

Hallam frowned and it seemed to take him a moment or two to realise that she had changed the subject. 'She's all right,' he answered eventually. 'She's gone home to her parents in Paris for a few weeks until she gets the cast off.'

He did not seem unduly disturbed by the news so Abby guessed that he wasn't interested in her in the way she had thought. Maybe Jaime fancied him, but then what girl wouldn't? Vicki was a prime example. And herself! What had this man got that every woman fell in love with him? She closed her eyes wearily. Why was everything such a mess?

'There's something I have to say to you, Abby,' he said after what seemed like an eternity. 'Though whether this is the right time I'm not really sure.'

His quiet voice made her look at him again.

'It will probably embarrass you but it's important to me that you know.'

Hope began to materialise, a distant singing, like a choir of angels reaching her all the way from heaven. Her heart thumped unsteadily. 'I'm listening,' she said softly.

If he did declare his love then her every dream would come true. If he didn't then pride would help her keep her head high and her unhappiness locked in her heart. It would have to.

'I love you, Abby.'

'I beg your pardon?' She had not expected him to make his declaration quite so clearly and so loudly—and so proudly.

'I love you,' he said again, but there was a faint hesitancy now, as though he knew she had heard him the first time and was trying to sort out what to say, how to tell him that she did not return his feelings.

'It doesn't make sense,' she whispered.

'It does to me,' he told her quietly, huskily. 'They're the truest words I've ever spoken.' He leaned forward to kiss her—a gentle, hesitant kiss, giving Abby every opportunity to deny him if she wanted to.

She didn't. His announcement was music in her ears—what she had wanted and hoped for and thought would never happen. She could sense now the hunger he was holding back, the fear that he would frighten her and cause her to lash out at him with angry words. There had been enough of those!

And when she remained silent he looked desperately

worried. 'I had to say it, Abby. I didn't want you to
think bad of me for the rest of your life. I didn't want
you to think that I made love to you for the sheer hell
of it. Why do you think I stopped myself so often? I
couldn't do that to you. It would have been unfair.'

Abby wondered whether now was the time to say she
loved him too, and decided it wasn't. There were a few
things she wanted to find out about him before commit-
ting herself. 'Do you mind if I ask you something?'

'Go ahead,' he said at once.

'Why did your wife leave you for another man?'

This was something he had obviously not expected
and he gave himself a tiny shake before answering.
'That's a question I've asked myself many times. I can
assure you I was a good husband to her, Abby. It wasn't
because I ill-treated her or anything like that.'

'Did you love her?'

He nodded. 'Though only time has taught me that
perhaps I got married too young; I was only nineteen.
Love holds different values; I found that out as I got
older. What I feel for you cannot be compared with what
I felt for Fiona.'

Abby felt pleased about that.

'She's part of the reason I gave you a hard time.'

Abby frowned, and then decided it hurt too much and
closed her eyes instead.

'She was a solicitor too,' he said, 'and the guy she
ran off with was one of the partners in her practice.'

A lot of things became clear when he said that. 'So
you assumed all solicitors were the same?'

'Yes,' he agreed wryly, 'and not only them. I tarred
all professional women with the same brush. I've seen
it happen too many times.'

'And you thought, because I let you kiss me, because

I gave away the fact that you were able to arouse me all too easily, that I was just as promiscuous?'

His guilty expression gave him away. 'I actually took advantage of it, much to my disgust now.'

'Why didn't you want me to come to France in the first place?' It was a question that had all too frequently puzzled her.

Hallam pulled a wry face. 'Fear. Pure, unadulterated fear.'

'Of what?' she asked with a frown.

'My own feelings,' he confessed. 'My inability to keep my hands off you. I think I loved you right from the word go. I'd never met such a spunky lady in all my life. You entranced me; you captivated me.'

Abby's heart sang sweet and loud—but she had not finished yet. 'How about Vicki Duvall? What are your feelings for her?'

He looked astonished that she should have brought Vicki into the conversation as well. 'She's a nice kid but that's all.'

'She has a crush on you—a major crush.'

'Maybe,' he agreed, 'but I've certainly never given her any encouragement; you can rest assured about that. And with a bit of luck it would appear that she has turned her affections to my son.'

'And do you mind that?'

'Goodness, no,' he said. 'They're the right age for each other, they should have plenty of fun together, and it will certainly get her off my back.'

'Hasn't she met Greg before?'

Hallam shook his head, and then, as a fleeting thought came into his mind, added, 'He wants to be a gemmologist, can you believe that?' His eyes danced with delight. 'I have a lot to thank you for.'

'So have I.' Greg suddenly came into the room. 'Abby, how are you? My father left a note; I just found it. The party went on for hours, I'm afraid. I've been worried sick all the way here.'

'I'll live,' she told him cheerfully, extricating her hand from Hallam's. 'It was just a little knock.' And she wondered whether he and Vicki had had a private party afterwards. He certainly looked very pleased with himself.

'Not so little by the look of you,' he said. 'What happened exactly?'

Abby explained how she had slipped, not saying that it had been because she had been running away from Hallam. 'Thank goodness your father saved me.'

Then she looked at Hallam. 'Exactly what were you doing there?' It had puzzled her how he had been in the right spot at the right time. Thank goodness he had been—she would have drowned otherwise—but it nevertheless remained a mystery.

His lips twisted wryly. 'I'm afraid I followed you. I saw you slip out of the party; I was half expecting it, as a matter of fact, but I didn't expect you to go down to the beach. I was watching you when you slipped. And thank goodness I was,' he finished strongly.

'I'll say,' breathed Greg. 'Goodness, I hate to think what could have happened if you hadn't been there. What ever possessed you to go climbing over those rocks at that time of night, Abby?'

'I needed some fresh air,' she answered hesitantly. 'That reminds me—how did you and Vicki get on? You seemed pretty wrapped in each other when I left.'

A smile split his face in two. 'We got on well. She's quite a girl. I'm taking her out this afternoon, when we've both caught up on some sleep, if that's all right with you, Father.'

'You're a free agent, son,' declared Hallam. 'Enjoy your holiday.'

Abby caught Greg's eye and he gave a grin. 'When I came in you two looked as though you were having a serious conversation,' he said. 'I think I'll get along and leave you to it. I'm glad you're not too badly hurt, Abby.'

'Thanks,' she said, and her eyes followed him to the door, where he turned and winked and Abby knew that she had his approval. When he was out of sight she smiled at Hallam. 'He really is a nice boy.'

Hallam nodded. 'I've underestimated him. And I'm sorry if I ever thought you were interested in Greg. I should have known that you were simply being friendly.' He grimaced ruefully. 'Now, where were we?' Her hand was taken again into his, his thumb stroking, his eyes intent on hers.

Abby's nerve-endings quivered. The time had come, she felt, to tell him about her own feelings. 'Would it interest you to know that no one else has ever managed to make me feel like you do?'

A faint frown drew his brows together. 'Are you trying to tell me something?'

She smiled and looked proudly into his eyes. 'That I love you too, Hallam Lane.'

'You do?' His voice registered disbelief, but he looked faintly hopeful at the same time.

She nodded. 'From the bottom of my heart.'

'Are you sure?'

'Perfectly sure,' she told him. 'Without you life would have no meaning.'

He shook his head. 'Why didn't you tell me sooner? Why didn't you give me a clue? Do you know what you've put me through?'

'I've suffered just as much,' she said.

'Impossible,' he declared, and the next second his arms were around her, careful because of her injury, but strong and possessive also. 'How long have you known?' he muttered as his mouth found hers.

'Actually only since yesterday afternoon,' she confessed. 'I thought all along it was a simple chemical attraction. I should have listened to Harriet.'

'Harriet?' he questioned. 'Harriet the barrister?'

Abby laughed at his incredulity. 'She told me I was in love with you. Of course I didn't believe her.'

'Then she's obviously a much more astute woman than you,' he told her strongly.

Their kiss was achingly beautiful—but far too short. He pulled away abruptly and she looked at him with a puzzled frown, until he said, 'I want you to marry me, Sommers.'

It was such a bald statement that she laughed. 'I could never marry a man who calls me Sommers,' she asserted primly.

'Than I'll call you Abby,' he agreed. 'But to me you'll always be Sommers. My beautiful, charming, adorable Sommers. Solicitor *extraordinaire*.'

'Is that a proposal?' she enquired, thoroughly thrilled at the thought of marrying this man whom she loved unreservedly.

'Proposal be damned,' he answered. 'I'm telling you, woman: you're marrying me; there's no doubt about it. I'm not letting you escape.' He paused a moment and then added, 'It's strange, but it never occurred to me to question why you were so willing. Maybe if I had then I would have realised that you loved me too. I would never have seen red because I found you in Rod Duvall's arms. What was that all about, by the way?'

Abby pulled her lips down at the corners. 'I sought consolation because I'd seen the welcome you gave Vicki—and the one she gave you. It sure looked as though you were—very fond of each other.'

'I treat her as a sister, that's all,' he told her with an insouciant shrug.

'Then why didn't you want to go to the party?' she enquired.

'Hell, Sommers, I thought your job depended on your ferreting out the truth? Couldn't you see that it was because I was jealous? I didn't want you there in case I lost you to Rod. I already knew that he was attracted to you. He made no secret of it.'

'And when you found us together your worst fears were realised?'

He inclined his head.

'You worried unnecessarily,' she said with a gentle smile. 'I'd already made it clear to him that I wanted no involvement.'

'But I didn't know that, did I?' he groaned. 'What a mess I've made of everything.'

'For no longer,' she assured him, and this time it was her turn to kiss him. Confidently now she raised her lips to his, pressing her whole body close, declaring her love in the best way she knew how. Even the pain in her head had gone for the moment.

'I have to be the luckiest man in the world,' he said raggedly.

'And I the luckiest woman,' she insisted.

'Wait till I tell Greg; he'll be so surprised.'

'Somehow I think he already knows,' murmured Abby. 'He's much more discerning than you think. I wonder if the hospital would object if you slid into bed with me?'

'Sommers!'

'Yes, Mr Lane?'

'I adore you. But let's wait until we're married.'

Her brows lifted, and she wondered how they could restrain themselves for so long.

But before she could even say a word he added, 'As soon as possible. By special licence. I'll go and organise things now. Just lie there, my sweet, and get better.' He sprang off the bed and was across the room in two strides. At the door he turned. 'My adorable, beautiful Sommers, I love you.

'And I love you,' she said, slipping back down between the sheets and closing her eyes. She was happy—completely happy. And soon she would be happier. Soon she would become Mrs Hallam Lane. How good it sounded. And she knew without a shadow of doubt that she was doing the right thing. Hallam was the man for her, for ever and ever and ever.

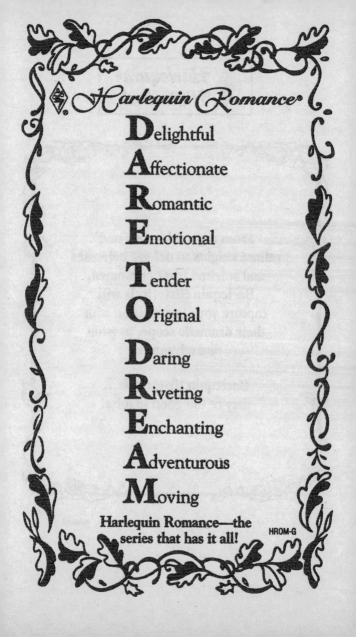

Harlequin Romance®

Delightful
Affectionate
Romantic
Emotional
Tender
Original
Daring
Riveting
Enchanting
Adventurous
Moving

Harlequin Romance—the
series that has it all!

HROM-G

Harlequin® Historical

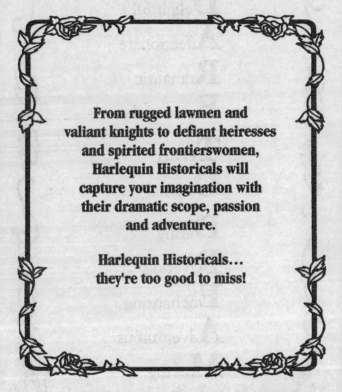

From rugged lawmen and
valiant knights to defiant heiresses
and spirited frontierswomen,
Harlequin Historicals will
capture your imagination with
their dramatic scope, passion
and adventure.

Harlequin Historicals...
they're too good to miss!

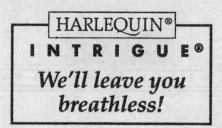

HARLEQUIN®

I N T R I G U E®

We'll leave you breathless!

If you've been looking for thrilling tales of
contemporary passion and sensuous love stories
with taut, edge-of-the-seat suspense—
then you'll *love* **Harlequin Intrigue!**

Every month, you'll meet four new heroes
who are guaranteed to make your spine tingle
and your pulse pound. With them you'll enter
into the exciting world of Harlequin Intrigue—
where your life is on the line
and so is your heart!

THAT'S INTRIGUE—DYNAMIC
ROMANCE AT ITS BEST!

HARLEQUIN®

I N T R I G U E®

LOOK FOR OUR FOUR FABULOUS MEN!

Each month some of today's bestselling authors bring
four new fabulous men to Harlequin American Romance.
Whether they're rebel ranchers, millionaire power brokers
or sexy single dads, they're all gallant princes—and
they're all ready to sweep you into lighthearted fantasies
and contemporary fairy tales where anything is possible
and where all your dreams come true!

You don't even have to make a wish…
Harlequin American Romance will grant your every desire!

Look for Harlequin American Romance
wherever Harlequin books are sold!

HARLEQUIN SUPERROMANCE®

...there's more to the story!

Superromance. A *big* satisfying read about unforget-
table characters. Each month we offer
four very different stories that range from family
drama to adventure and mystery, from highly emotional stories to romantic comedies—and
much more! Stories about people you'll
believe in and care about. Stories too
compelling to put down....

Our authors are among today's *best* romance writ-
ers. You'll find familiar names and
talented newcomers. Many of them are
award winners—and you'll see why!

If you want the biggest and best
in romance fiction, you'll get it
from Superromance!

Available wherever Harlequin books are sold.

Look us up on-line at: http://www.romance.net

HS-GEN